Forging Blade

Charon MC
Book 11

KHLOE WREN

Books by Khloe Wren

Charon MC:
Inking Eagle
Fighting Mac
Chasing Taz
Claiming Tiny
Chasing Scout
Tripping Nitro
Scout's Legacy
Mac's Destiny
Losing Bash
Finding Needles
Forging Blade

Fire and Snow:
Guardian's Heart
Noble Guardian
Guardian's Shadow
Fierce Guardian
Necessary Alpha
Protective Instincts

Dragon Warriors:
Enchanting Eilagh
Binding Becky
Claiming Carina
Seducing Skye
Believing Binda

Jaguar Secrets:
Jaguar Secrets
FireStarter

Other Titles:
Fireworks
Tigers Are Forever
Bad Alpha Anthology
Scarred Perfection
Scandals: Zeck
Mirror Image Seduction
Deception
Mine To Bear

ISBN: 978-0-6486896-3-8

Cover Credits:
Model: Robert Kelly
Photographer: Jean Woodfin of JW Photography and Covers
Digital Artist: Khloe Wren
Editing Credits:
Editor: Carolyn Depew of Write Right

Acknowledgements

As always, my wonderful husband and kids get the first round of thanks. They always support me and help me get my stories written. I'm extremely blessed to have such a wonderful family.

To my editor, Carolyn, thank you for the continuous support and assistance with so much more than just editing.

A huge thanks to Jo Carol and Johnny, along with Stacey and Claudia for your help with various research on this one. My PA Andrea Rhoads, thank you for once more doing what you do! Fiona G, woman, your skills have turned things around for me, I can't thank you enough.

My Night Writer sprint buddies, I can't thank you all enough for keeping me going. And of course, my street team, thank you ladies for all your words of encouragement.

Just this once, I got the book written with enough time for my betas to read it! Thanks Andrea, Vicki, Stacey and Miranda for helping get this baby all polished up.

Lastly, to you who's reading this. Thank you so much for taking a chance with me and I hope you enjoy reading Forging Blade as much as I did writing it.

xo

Khloe Wren

PS. You know how authors say we get even in our writing? It's not a joke, people. Elita was the meanest of mean girls who made my life hell back in my late primary and early high school years. So, when you get to her demise, just know: She's had it coming for over 25 years now.

Biography

Khloe Wren lives in rural South Australia with her husband, two daughters and an ever changing list of animals!

She started writing in 2013 and has published over 30 books since then in the romantic suspense genre. She writes both paranormal and contemporary stories, including her best selling series Charon MC.

Khloe enjoys writing outside of the box and she loves her heroes strong, and her heroines even stronger.

Charon:

Char·on \ˈsher-ən, ˈker-ən, -än\

In Greek mythology, the Charon is the ferryman who takes the dead across either the river Styx or Acheron, depending on whether the soul's destination is the Elysian Fields or Hades.

Chapter 1

Blade

Every step down the hallway had my rage boiling hotter. In my soul, I knew the room of kids we'd just found wasn't going to be the worst thing I saw today.

Together with a handful of Charon MC men, I was cracking open the L.A. mob's stable. Technically, it was my boss', Antonio Sabella's, business I was about to help destroy, but considering I'd just come from putting that fucker in the ground, I was guessing I could comfortably say that he was my previous boss and that I was definitely now out of the mob. Finally, I was free from my cage.

My mind was still spinning at what we'd discovered in that first room we'd opened up. The smell had been bad enough I'd nearly gagged, but the sight of all those kids was something that will haunt me for years. I cleared my throat past the lump that was still lodged there. Boys and girls, some just toddlers, had all been huddled together in that room. They'd all tried to get away from the door when it had opened, all except one. A teenage girl had stood strong, ready to fight.

I mentally shook my head at how gutsy the kid was. They'd all shown clear signs that they'd been abused. Their naked bodies told stories that should never have been written. Yet that teen hadn't cowered, hadn't tried to hide. Instead, she'd demanded a weapon to defend the others in case we didn't make it back to her as we told her we would. That kid was way too calm for what she'd been through. I was fairly certain I wouldn't have been that fucking calm in her shoes. Not that she was wearing any.

The sight of all those kids was enough to trigger my fury on its own, but my rage had been churning since long before I stepped foot in that room. Before we'd ended Antonio Sabella's miserable life earlier, he'd told me he had suspected I might have been trying something when I arranged the meeting for today, so he had handed my girl over to his men to enjoy while he'd come to meet us. Fucker had thought I'd spare his life so he could call and have his men stop their games with her. Stupid bastard forgot I'd been trained under his reign. I knew full well he wouldn't have made that call no matter what happened. Once he'd handed her over, her fate had been sealed as far as he'd been concerned. I was here to attempt to change it. The sounds of men enjoying sex echoed around the hallway as we marched toward the source of all the noise. With every step, I was praying we were going to be in time to save her.

I didn't need to see through the walls to know she was in that room. Deep down, I knew. I fucking knew that those men had my Josefina in there. Sabella had kept her all to himself for seventeen fucking years, apparently not allowing anyone else to abuse her. By doing that, he'd made her into an unattainable object. So today, when, before he'd come to meet with me, he'd told his men they could take her and have their fun with her, they would have jumped at the chance. They'd have been worked up and been doing the vilest of things to their boss' favorite toy.

I'd first met Josefina when I was twenty-one. She'd been a kid, just sixteen years old. Unfortunately for her, she'd already had an adult's body. Lush breasts to go with her curvy hips and ass. She was a young man's wet dream, but I hadn't gotten aroused when I'd first seen her.

Antonio had sent me and another of his men, Gino, out to collect protection money from a few places when we'd found her. Her clothes had been torn up and she'd clearly been recently drugged. Gino, the fucker, had made a comment about easy pussy and had moved to grab her. Before I knew what I was doing, I'd growled out a claim on her, making threats to kill Gino if he dared to touch her.

At six feet, I was only slightly taller than Gino, but I easily outweighed him in muscle. Since being forced into the mob, I'd focused on keeping myself not only strong, but skilled in how to fight. There weren't many men around who would even try to take me on, which was why Gino had not even attempted to argue with me. With a laugh, he'd backed off and told me to have fun, that he could wait till I was done to have his shot at such a pretty puta. I'd grabbed the clearly frightened girl and dragged her off with me, leaving Gino to do the rest of the collections for the day on his own.

I knew he'd assumed I was taking her some place to fuck her, but that had never been my intention. Never once did I touch her in a sexual manner. From the first moment, I saw her as a little sister. A scared, lost, little girl who needed protecting. I'd taken her back to my small apartment and told her she was safe. That I wouldn't hurt her. I'd grabbed one of my clean shirts, a pair of boxers and guided her to my bathroom.

It had taken her a few days before she stopped jumping every time she saw me. Before she believed that I wasn't going to hurt her. She only knew a few English words so I'd been grateful that I'd paid attention during Spanish classes in school. Still, it had taken over a month before she'd trusted me enough to answer my questions about how she'd come to be on that street where we'd met.

She'd finally confessed to me that she'd been snatched from her parents' farm in northern Mexico by a local gang and sold to a white man. By the time she'd finished her story I knew we were both fucked. Sabella had been testing me, seeing if I'd fuck her then bring her in like he thought I should have. But I hadn't.

Three months later, I'd come home to find my place had been trashed and Josefina gone. I'd known who'd done it and I'd gone directly to Sabella to call him on it. Fucker had simply shrugged his shoulders and told me he'd paid good money for the girl and had simply taken back what was his before he moved his merchandise. He'd also informed me she hadn't survived the trip to her new owner and was now dead.

I'd never wanted to kill the man more than I had in that moment, but I couldn't fucking touch him. If I did, my old man would take it out on my mother and my little brother. I couldn't risk their lives like that. Especially since I'd believed Josefina was already dead. But it hadn't stopped me from setting up a long-range plan for revenge.

"Everyone loaded and ready?"

I was pulled from the past by Mac's deep and steady voice. We'd all stopped in front of the door where the noise was coming from. Like the other men, I pulled my gun. Checked the safety was off then put my hand, not holding my weapon, to the grip and waited for Mac to give me the word.

"Do it, Blade."

I'd shoved the door wide open and lifted my gun, took aim at Gino, who had been enjoying finally getting a chance with Josefina, and shot my former colleague through the middle of his fucking forehead. The others all took their shots too, and a thunder of sound filled the small room, making my ears ring.

Men dropped like flies until only one stood. I didn't recognize the fucker. He had Josefina's naked body pulled up in front of him, a knife to her throat. I'd purposefully not looked at her first, because I knew I'd lose my mind at the sight. And I'd been right. She'd matured over the years, grown more beautiful. Even through the blood and bruises covering her naked body I could see what she should look like. Her head and torso were off the table, blocking the fucker holding her while her legs lay listless on the surface she'd been violated on. She blinked as she looked straight through me. Her eyes were lifeless and saw nothing.

My heart shattered into a thousand pieces, my soul cried out in agony. She'd never done anything wrong in her life. Why did she have to suffer so damn much? Without thought, I released a scream as I lunged toward her. She was still alive, though. So long as she breathed I could fix her. Find help to get her put back together again. She could still live her life, if I could just get to her…

Mac's thick arm curled around my shoulders, pulling me back against his solid frame.

"Stop and think. He'll kill her."

A noise left my throat that I didn't recognize as I watched helplessly as her skin grew paler, the bruises grew darker and the blood trailing down her thighs now dripped to the floor.

I jerked against Mac's hold when Eagle came out of nowhere and slammed a blade into the back of the fucker's neck, killing him instantly. It was too good for the bastard. He deserved to suffer, but not at the risk of making Josefina suffer more than she already had. At the same time that Eagle caught Josefina as she fell, Mac released me. I bolted across the small room, taking her from Eagle before dropping to the floor with her cradled against me.

I gently stroked her face and rested my forehead against hers before I whispered to her in Spanish.

"I'm sorry, Josefina. So fucking sorry. I didn't know. He told me you were dead. I would have come for you sooner. Fuck, I shouldn't have left you at my place unprotected like that."

"Not your fault. You helped me. Did all you could. Not your fault." She paused to take a breath that rattled in her chest. "He was right. I died years ago. Nothing left now."

Her words were a quiet rasp, barely discernable. With a sigh, her body went still, no longer breathing, but I couldn't move. I'd been too late to save her. She was dead, killed in a brutal way after years of torture and it was all my fucking fault.

I didn't flinch when Mac crouched beside me. Mac and I had been colleagues for a time. Antonio had blackmailed both of us into this mess. Mac had been smarter than me, though. He'd enlisted in the USMC to get out of Sabella's hands. Pity that hadn't been an option for me. My old man made sure I'd known it, too. Mac reached over her body, pressing his fingers to her neck in search of a pulse. I knew what he'd find, or rather, not find.

"Don't say it."

"I'm sorry, brother. But we gotta keep moving. We need to find the other women and any other men who are here. We can lock you in here and come back for you—"

I shook my head, cutting him off. I wasn't going to be like those kids. Locked away, waiting for someone to return to tell me it was all done. "I want blood for this. No way am I going to sit this one out."

Rising to my feet, I laid her out on the table as though she were still breathing, kissed her temple and ignored the tears that ran down my face as I whispered my final words to her.

"Rest easy, baby. It's over now."

Guilt and rage fogged my mind and fueled my actions as we'd cleared out the rest of the warehouse. I was on edge, looking for an outlet, but we found no more guards. Which, considering how many had been in with Josefina, I guess made sense. There had been a few johns in with the women, making the most of being unsupervised. But those fuckers barely put up a fight. I needed something more than taking down a couple cowards to burn off my rage. I managed to bank my fury as we uncuffed the women and helped them out of the warehouse. They'd all been through enough, last thing they needed was to fear their rescuers.

When we had almost all the women and kids free of the building, Mac had me call in the authorities. I'd already made contact with a cop I knew was clean in anticipation of what we were going to find here. So I walked away from the others and dialed her number.

"Lopez."

"It's bigger than we thought. Haven't done a solid head count, but you've got at least twenty women and nearly that many kids. They're all in a bad way. Gonna need a few buses."

"Any life threatening injuries?"

My fucking eyes stung as I wished I could answer her yes. That Josefina was alive. I cleared my throat. "No. Nothing life threatening. There's one woman who didn't make it. We weren't fast enough to save her." My fucking voice cracked and I cleared my throat again. "There's several of Sabella's men too. We've left 'em where they fell. We've got all the women and kids out in the parking lot."

"Why'd you put them outside?"

Lopez's voice was firm but I knew the shit I was telling her was affecting her. No matter how weathered a cop was, this shit was going to leave a mark.

"Gonna light the fucking office up. Can't risk someone finding enough information to start this shit back up again."

"That paperwork might be the evidence we need to put Sabella away, along with the rest of his crew. Might be the only way to identify the victims."

Yeah, I wasn't going to tell her that she didn't need to worry about Sabella ever again.

"The only one that can't talk is Josefina Chavez. She was snatched from her parents' farm in Mexico when she was sixteen, back in 2001. All the others will be able to tell you who they are. I'm not risking that information getting into the wrong hands and this pipeline starting up again."

She was quiet for a moment. I knew she wasn't happy, but I also knew she got what I was saying. The world would be a nicer place without this shit in it. "You've got about twenty minutes, then I'll be rolling in with a team. I'm not going to actively come looking for you, and I'll put through this tip as one given anonymously, but if evidence is found to implicate you and you're found, you'll go down for this. Nothing I can do about that. Just like there'll be others who will be gunning for you. I'd suggest you leave town for a while. In your shoes, I'd be leaving California for good."

She hung up before I could say another word and I headed back toward Mac to tell him our time limit. Then I headed over to the Charon's van to get the can of gas. I didn't waste time getting back inside to that fucking office filled with documentation of all the evil deeds Sabella had processed through the place. With my nose pressed against my shoulder to curb the smell, I poured gas around the office. There was a shit ton of paperwork in here and I didn't want to risk the wrong people getting any of it and working out how to import more women and kids from across the border. Not that everyone we'd found here was Mexican. Plenty of locals had been caught up in this mess too.

Josefina's face filled my vision as I poured and my hand slipped, splashing the flammable liquid over it and up my wrist, along with down my side.

"Fuck."

Tossing the can aside, I shook the liquid off my hand before wiping it on my jeans. Then I pulled an old-school book of matches from my pocket and struck one. Watching the flame burn, I let it mesmerize me for a few moments before I flicked it toward the desk. All the gas I'd poured around the room couldn't wait to light up and I quickly realized I'd used way too much. The overkill had been intentional, I hadn't wanted anything in here to be left unburned. I just hadn't fully thought the plan through.

A spark came my way and out of reflex, I attempted to bat it away, forgetting about my fuel-soaked skin and clothing.

"Motherfucker!"

I backpeddled from the room, turning my head away from my side that now had flames licking up it. Pain lit me up faster than the fire.

"Fuck."

I'd barely heard Mac's curse before he'd thrown a blanket over me and knocked me to the ground, rolling me until the flames were out.

Agony stole my vision, my ability to think. I was vaguely aware of Mac tossing me over his shoulder before he took off. Each step jolted my burns and more pain shot through me. By the time he laid me out on the seats in the rear of the van, I was clenching my jaw so I didn't throw up from the intensity of my agony.

"We'll get you taken care of, brother."

I gave him a jerky nod, hoping he didn't ask me anything else. I didn't want to fucking talk. My mind was still shorting out due to the fucking pain. I'd never felt anything like it.

Bright lights streamed in the windows and the door slid open to reveal they'd brought me to a hospital. At least with all the wildfires currently burning throughout southern California, we shouldn't get too many questions about how I'd gotten injured.

"No way to do this without it hurting, Blade."

I unlocked my jaw. "Just do it already."

With any luck, I'd black the fuck out and wouldn't feel any more pain.

It was all a blur as I was taken into the ER and hooked up to a drip. I let Mac do the talking as I stared up at ceiling. But it wasn't aging sheetrock that I saw. It was Josefina. Her battered face and body, her hollow eyes.

"He was right. I died years ago. Nothing left now."

For seventeen years, Sabella had been using and abusing her. I doubted I could imagine the torture he'd inflicted upon her. That poor girl. She'd never done a thing to deserve it. Her parents had been poor farmers who'd been unfortunate enough to have been blessed with a beautiful daughter.

That had me thinking of my own parents. My mother had been wonderful, but she'd been limited by the ruthless bastard she'd married. I'd gotten her free of him, though. It had taken time, but I'd managed to get my mother and brother away from my brute of a father. Then I'd taken care of my old man once and for all. Just like Sabella, I'd done it on the sly, so no one had known it was me. And also like Sabella, that bastard had died hard, but not hard enough for what he'd done to those he was meant to have loved and cherished.

I'd never understood how my old man could have done it. Sold his child, his first born son, to the mob. He'd run a small jewelry store and hadn't wanted to pay the protection fee, so instead, he'd bartered for it by giving me to Sabella. Even at sixteen I'd been a big kid, strong and stubborn. So Sabella had been more than happy to take me, especially when he'd overheard my father's threat against my mother and brother should I not follow orders. He'd known he could do what he pleased with me then, mold me into who he needed me to be. Pity for him that his plan backfired on him.

I hissed in pain as the doctor examined a particularly sore burn.

"Hmm, yes, definitely an area of third degree but mostly first and second degree. I'll get the nurse in here to tend to them. She'll tell you what you need to know about taking care of them."

The look on this guy's face and the way he curled his lip as he pulled his gloves off and tossed them in the bin basically told me he considered me no better than dirt beneath his shoe and clearly not worth his time. That shit pissed me right off. Considering the edge I was still on after what went down, it was probably a good thing Mac had stripped my gun off me before he'd brought me in. And was sitting beside me to run interference.

Despite wanting to teach this guy a fucking lesson, I managed to force myself to stay quiet. It helped that I wanted him to fuck off away from me more than I wanted to pound him into the ground.

He stepped away from my bed and shoving the curtain open, flagged down a nurse like she was a cab. What the fuck was this guy's issue? The nurse had a neutral, professional expression that said she didn't like the prick any more than I did. Their conversation was quick and I was certain I caught her sighing with relief when he stepped away from her and she came into my little slice of the ER.

"He an asshole to everyone or are we just special?"

She snorted a laugh. "Dr. Maestro? He treats everyone equally, that one. Unless you have money pouring off you."

Mac shook his head, pulling my attention to where he sat beside my bed. He'd been so quiet, I'd nearly forgotten he was there. He was still giving me a strange look, as though he was waiting for me to do something stupid.

"So, ma'am, what's the damage and what do we need to do to keep him healthy?"

She gave Mac a smile. "Please, call me Lilly." She turned to face me, rolling a cart with bandages and shit with her.

"You were quite lucky, Mr. Walker. Your thick jeans saved your legs from receiving more serious burns, and your friend's quick thinking with the blanket quite possibly saved your arm, if not your life."

Mac cleared his throat as he shuffled around in the hard seat, like he was uncomfortable with the praise. I switched my attention back to the nurse, Lilly, but struggled to track what she was saying. I was still in enough pain that it was hard to focus for long, and after her earlier words, I found myself staring at the blistered skin of my arm, thinking about what would have happened if Mac hadn't come to my rescue when he had. Could I really have lost my arm in that fire? Or even my life?

Spilling that gas had been an accident. Yeah, losing Josefina in such a horrific way had cut me to the core. And it was going to take me some time to wrap my head around it all. I was probably going to be seeing her battered body in my nightmares for years. I knew what Mac was thinking, that it wasn't an accident. But at no point today did I want to join her in death, and especially not by fire. If I was going to end things, I'd find something faster and less painful than fucking burning to death.

Blade

No matter how fast I ran, I couldn't get to her. I reached out to grab her, to pull her free of the torment, but she stayed out of reach.

Antonio stood over her writhing, battered body, laughing at me trying to reach her.

"She was never yours, boy. She was a test that you failed. It's your fault." He spread his hands out, indicating Josefina's body, covered with bleeding welts and bruises. "This is all your fault."

"No! Release her!"

I screamed out as he continued to chant the words, "It's all your fault".

"Blade! Wake up, man."

The horrific images and the sound of Antonio's voice faded at the intrusion of Mac's deep voice.

I went to rub my face, but stopped with a wince when my fingers touched a tender part of my cheek that had caught a lick of the flames yesterday.

Blinking the last traces of the nightmare from my mind, I looked up at Mac's expression. He looked serious, like he was on a mission.

"What's going on?"

"We got a lot to discuss, and not a whole lot of time at the moment to do it, so I'm gonna keep it brief. I'm not comfortable leaving you alone right now. I don't like where your head's at after yesterday. I wish I could offer to stay here with you, but that's a no go. Got word from home last night that my baby girl's been in the hospital. I need to get home to my family and I want you to come with us."

I winced and turned from him, staring up at the water stains on the ceiling. Once he and the other Charons left, I'd be alone. I knew I had to disappear after what had happened yesterday. I didn't know what Sabella's remaining men would do with his disappearance. I had no clue who knew he was coming to meet me other than those we'd killed already. But like Officer Lopez told me, I needed to leave town. But I wasn't a fucking moron. I knew it was highly likely fallout from putting Sabella in the ground was going to find me no matter where I went. Did I want to bring that down on the Charon MC? Especially on Mac and his family? He'd just reminded me of the fact he had a wife and baby. It wouldn't be fair to risk them. Not for me. I wasn't worth it.

"I ain't one of you, Mac. I don't belong—"

"Bull fucking shit, Blade! You belong. You've helped out the Charons more than once. I have Scout's blessing to bring you back to Bridgewater. He told me it was up to you if you wanted to join the club, but even if you don't, you're welcome in our town. My old lady told me last night to bring you home so we could look after you."

I turned to look him in the eye to gauge if he was speaking the truth. Had Scout, the Charon MC president, really given his blessing to have me in his town? He would know the risk I posed to his club and everyone around him simply by my presence in their vicinity. And Mac had asked his old lady, his wife, if she was okay with having me in their home, of all places? That, I couldn't do. I couldn't put Mac's wife and baby at that much risk.

Mac continued speaking. "You're not alone, brother. Let us help you. Once your burns heal up, we'll revisit where you want to live going forward. If you want to come back here, you can. If you don't, we'll help you move all your shit to Bridgewater."

I stayed silent for a few more moments as I absorbed what Mac appeared to be offering me. It seemed too good to be true. And I'd learned the hard way, more than once, that things that seemed that way generally were.

"What's up with your kid?"

"Allergic reaction to amoxicillin. Zara got her to a hospital in time so she'll be fine, but I wanna get back home to them to see for myself."

I winced. No wonder he was all business about getting back home. Before I could say another word, the young club prospect, Jazz, came thundering through the trailer like his ass was on fire.

"We got a problem, Mac. A big, fucking problem."

Mac reached for his gun and I forced my body to sit up, spinning my legs over the side of the bed. If trouble had arrived, I wasn't going to get caught with nothing but my dick in my hand.

"Spill it, Jazz. What the fuck's going on?"

The prospect eyed Mac prepping his weapon for use as he moved toward the bedroom door.

"Nothing that needs a gun. At least I hope that's not the route we're taking…"

Their voices faded slightly as they moved out of the room, but the trailer was small and had thin walls, so I could still hear them as I gritted my teeth and stood. I kept the string of curses at the pain that flared through my right side in my head silent. The nurse had given me some hardcore painkillers to take last night and they'd knocked me out all night, but this morning they'd worn off completely and I was hurting like a son of a bitch.

"Jazz. Cut the shit. What is the problem?"

"We got a stowaway. That teenager from the warehouse—the one you gave your shirt to—well, she's asleep in the back of the van."

"She still sleeping?"

"Yeah. I saw her through the window as I was about to open things up. Figured I'd get you before I risked waking her."

Ah, fuck. There'd only been one teen in that fucked up place. The one who had demanded a weapon to protect the other kids when we had to lock them back in their filthy room. She'd had a look in her eye that had reminded me of Josefina, of myself. The look of a fighter who'd been tested to the extreme, but was still there and still ready to go another round or two.

Unsure what Mac would do with her, I ignored my pain and dressed before heading outside with everyone else.

"Open it up, Jazz. Let's get this dealt with."

Jazz swung the door open, and with a jerk, the girl tried to hide under the pile of blankets that she'd clearly used as cover last night.

"We know you're there, darlin'."

Silently, she ran her gaze over each of us before settling it back on Mac's face.

"Please. Don't send me back."

My spine stiffened. I might not know what Mac was going to do, but I was one hundred fucking percent sure what he wouldn't do. No way would any man here see anyone, let alone a child, return to a shit-hole like the one we'd pulled her out of yesterday.

The bite to Mac's voice confirmed he was equally insulted the kid would think he would do such a thing. "I'd never send anyone back to a place like that. We busted that shit wide open and burned it to the ground so no one could ever be sent back there."

She shook her head. "Not the warehouse, to the cops."

That had me frowning. What the fuck was going on that she was just as scared of the police as she was of the mob who'd put her in that warehouse?

Keeping control over the situation, Mac nodded his head toward the trailer. "How about you come on inside? Get cleaned up and get something to eat, then we'll discuss what the next step here is gonna be."

Bank cleared his throat, drawing all the attention his way.

"I'll head down to Walmart and grab her something to change into and some other stuff she'll need."

Mac nodded his way. "Good idea. Thanks, brother. What size are you, darlin'?"

She rattled off her digits and Bank gave her a nod. "I've got you covered, honey. Got a baby sister who's probably about your age."

With that, Bank headed to his bike and took off. Mac offered his palm to the girl.

"C'mon, kid. Let's get you inside and more comfortable."

I couldn't help but be impressed with how seamlessly the club handled shit. A teen stowaway wasn't on any of our agendas but they just rolled with it. Bank stepped up to get her supplies, Mac took control of the situation, lifting her easily into his strong arms when her knees buckled beneath her. Then he got her safely inside and in to the bathroom where she could clean up. By the state she was in, I'd hazard a guess it had been a good, long while since she'd seen a hot shower.

Images of Josefina when I'd first found her flashed through my mind. The men who'd first kidnapped her had already used her before they'd sold her to Sabella. Fuckers had called it training. In reality it had been nothing more than a horrific series of gang rapes. Then Sabella had simply dumped her on the street for me to find after he'd sampled the goods. What was left of her clothing wasn't much. Just like this teen, Josefina had had scabbed knuckles to go with her bruised and battered body. At sixteen, she'd tried to fight off grown men who were clearly much stronger and bigger than she'd been. She hadn't been able to save herself, but she'd valiantly tried. My heart tore open as I wondered how many years it had taken Sabella to break her spirit enough that she'd stopped fighting. I doubted she could have kept it up for seventeen fucking years.

After the teen closed herself in the bathroom, Mac moved to the table and I joined the others to sit around him.

"Yesterday I asked her if her mom was in the warehouse. She told me straight out she didn't give a fuck if she was, because that bitch was the one who'd sold her to Sabella to pay off a drug debt. Just now she told me her dad would kill her before he'd take her into his home. I saw the shudder run through her at the thought of her old man. What the fuck, brothers? I don't understand how parents can do that."

I clenched my teeth so hard I heard my jaw crack. This kid was tearing what remained of my soul to shreds. I knew just how she felt. How Mac felt. And even all these years later, I couldn't answer his question. Why would parents sell their child for monetary gain? I had no fucking clue. If I were ever lucky enough to be blessed with kids, I'd make sure they knew they were loved. Make sure they were protected at all times. I looked to the bathroom door, but it wasn't the trailer's shitty walls

I saw. Nope, it was my childhood home. A nice house in the 'burbs. My dad dragging me down the stairs toward the front door. I could have broken free, but the bastard was busy telling me all the ways he'd hurt my mother and little brother if I so much as spoke out of turn where I was going.

I'd had no clue what was going on. Mom was crying. Tears flowed down her pale cheeks as she kept a palm clamped over her mouth to contain the sounds of her sobs. There were three big men standing in the middle of the front room. All three wore suits, but the one in the middle was the one to watch. Even at sixteen, I knew Antonio Sabella owned the streets in this part of L.A.

I'd asked my father what was going on and he'd shaken me and told me to shut the fuck up. That I was Sabella's problem now, and he was deadly serious about me doing as I was told without giving any lip. That my mother and brother would pay the price if I didn't. Aaron was ten years my junior. At six, he was nothing more than a scared little boy clinging to our mother's skirts, trying to hide from everyone around him.

The sound of Bank's Harley rolling up out front pulled me from that memory and by the time he'd dropped the bags of stuff at the bathroom door and joined us, I knew what I had to do.

Rapping my knuckles on the table, I waited for Mac to look me in the eye.

"You want me to come back to Texas with you? Well, I'll do it, but only if we take her with us as well."

Mac could take the girl home to his wife and I'd stay at their clubhouse. That way, I limited the risk to his family, and that girl crying in the bathroom because she had a bag of new shit from fucking Walmart would have a nice fucking life. I vowed I would see that girl have a better life than either Josefina or I ever had.

Chapter 2

Veronica

After checking each window and door of my small house was locked—twice—I made my way out the side door to the attached garage. Before starting my car, I pulled my phone out and checked the feed from the cameras I'd set up around the outside of my home. Once I was certain no one was anywhere near the front of the house, I hit the button to lift the garage door, started the engine and drove forward. I stayed in the driveway, watching everything going on up and down the street as I waited for the garage door to close again.

Once it shut, I headed to the hospital for my shift. At least once I was within the hospital I could relax. Security was tight, and I knew if I got in trouble all I had to do was call out and I'd have all the help I needed.

At work I was safe. No way would he be able to get to me here. But on the drive in was another story. Every car

I didn't recognize had my heart rate speeding up and my paranoia reaching epic proportions.

I was used to the routine, though. For the seven years I'd been living in Bridgewater, I'd done the same thing. Always vigilant. Always careful. It was a lonely way to live, and there were times when it got to me. Whenever it got too bad, I'd head out with two of the other nurses, Sophie and Laura, to Styx—the local bar—to have a few drinks and ogle all the hot biker eye candy none of us would ever be brave enough to try to touch. One of the older nurses, Donna, was married to one of those bikers we ogled. Even though Keys had to be in his sixties now, he was still a damn fine looking man. A little rough around the edges, but life did that to a person. I wouldn't trust someone who didn't have a few scars by the time they'd made it that far through life. And I was sure the external ones weren't the only ones he'd have. Heaven knows I had more scars on my soul than anywhere else.

Relief poured through me as I made my way through the hospital's doors. It was always like that. And as I took my first deep breath of the day, I made my way toward the staff locker room to drop my bag off and get ready to start my shift in the ER.

Bridgewater was your typical mid-sized Texan town and had the usual daily injuries. The Charon MC, the bike club that ran the town, kept it mostly clean, so thankfully drug-related shit wasn't common. Although there were a few patients we saw who clearly had an issue with prescription drugs, the illegal kind didn't make an appearance very often at all. That suited me just fine. My first nursing position had been in Dallas and I'd learned fast that drugs made people extremely unpredictable and very fucking hard to treat.

I'd lasted about five years there, but then I'd seen one of his men in the ER and knew I hadn't gone far enough from home. I'd made sure he hadn't seen me and as soon as he was gone, I handed in my notice and started looking for a job in a smaller town, that was further away.

It'd been nearly twenty years since I'd seen him, but I'd never stopped looking over my shoulder. Never let my guard down. Because I knew, deep down, I was certain the moment I let my guard down, he'd be there, waiting for me.

With a sigh, I pushed those thoughts aside before I got lost in my past, closed my locker and headed out to start my work day. Everything about the morning was utterly normal, until he came in. Flanked by two men wearing Charon MC vests, the most beautifully broken man I'd ever laid eyes on came in to the ER's waiting room. I wasn't sure if the bikers were his friends or his guards, but the man didn't look happy.

The trio came up to the desk and Rhonda took his information. I was close enough to overhear. He had burns that needed checking and redressing. I rushed forward so I could be the nurse in charge of his case.

I grabbed the board, skim reading what Rhonda had written in case I hadn't caught everything he'd said before I walked out into the waiting room.

"Mr. Walker?"

He stood, along with the bikers, and I held my palm up. "Just Mr. Walker."

The bikers both looked to Mr. Walker with a raised eyebrow and when he nodded, they both sat back down, getting as comfortable as two big guys could in the small plastic chairs the hospital had installed in the waiting room. Guess they were friends, then. Either way, I didn't need two huge men taking up space back in the treatment bays. I turned and strode over to the doors into the ER, not needing to check if Mr. Walker was following me, because I could feel his presence behind me the entire way.

"Take a seat on the bed and let's get this ball rolling." In one, smooth move, he slid his lean frame up onto the bed until he was sitting on the edge of it, facing me. His crystal blue irises that were so filled with pain caught my gaze, and for a minute I was struck mute and dumb. I'd never seen such arresting blue eyes before. What would they look like heated with lust? Or laughter? Agony was currently reflected in those pretty baby blues and my chest ached in response. Which had me frowning as I looked away, breaking the connection between us. What the fuck was wrong with me? Hopefully it was just an indicator that I was overdue for a girls' night out. I'd never had, or wanted, a boyfriend. I'd seen what a man could do when he thought he owned a woman. That shit wasn't for me.

I cleared my throat and forced myself back on task.

"So, you had a whoops with a fire, huh?"

He gave me a nod and a smirk that I did not find sexy. Not at all.

"Yeah, I was over in California. Was a little late evacuating and got caught. Got lucky and just have some burns on my right arm."

He was shrugging out of his button down shirt before I could ask anything else. Doing my best to ignore the glorious sight of his muscles rippling beneath the tight tank that stretched across his torso, I peeled the previous dressings from his wounds carefully, grateful when they didn't stick at all.

"How many days ago did you receive the injury?"

"Three days. I went straight to the hospital after it happened. When I got released, I came to stay with some friends here. The nurse in L.A. told me to come in to get the burns checked after a couple days, so here I am."

I gave him a nod as I took a good look at his burns. They were healing well, but still had a way to go.

"Do you need to wear long sleeved shirts for work?"

He gave me a suspicious frown. "I don't understand why you need to know that."

I nodded toward his arm. "It's healing well, and if you can stick to wearing tanks, it won't need another dressing, but if you're going to keep wearing button downs like the one you have on now, I'll redress it so it won't stick to your clothing if any of those blisters burst on you."

His big body relaxed and his expression cleared. "You'd best redress it. Does that mean I get to come in and see you again to redo the dressings?"

With a grin, I shook my head at his flirty tone. It was nothing unusual to have patients try to charm me, but it was a first that I was affected by it. There was something about the sorrow in this man's eyes that had drawn me in the moment I'd looked into them.

"I'm sure you can handle it from here. Just head into a pharmacy to get another burn dressing if you need to redo things. Leave it open to the air as much as you can. Give nature a chance to do its thing."

It was a few minutes later, as I was taping down the last edge of the new bandages, that he reached out with his good hand and touched me. My entire body went stiff and on alert, my breath stuttered as his fingertip lightly traced over my cheek, tucking a lock of hair that had escaped my bun behind my ear before his hand dropped away from me. I licked my lips, trying to get my heart rate to lower and my fucking brain to start working again.

I couldn't have a panic attack at work. Not just because a man startled me by touching my cheek. Especially when the man couldn't know my past, couldn't know what I'd suffered under gentle hands before.

Blade

Fuck, I'd not only scared her but hit some kind of trigger for her. The lovely nurse who had been so carefully tending my burns was the prettiest thing I'd seen in a long time. She had thick, dark brown hair that she'd pulled back into a knot thing at the back of her head, but a few strands had come lose and hung around her face. I'd been so damn curious as to whether her skin was as soft as it looked, that I'd reached out to her without thought. My fingertip had met pure silk when I'd run it over her cheekbone, before I hooked those strands and tucked them behind her ear. Mesmerized by her, I hadn't realized until then that my actions had scared the hell out of the poor woman. Her body was still as a stone as her breath stuttered in and out.

"Shit, I'm sorry. That was way out of line. I shouldn't have touched you without asking."

Her body was frozen still, midway through taping down the last of the dressings over my burns. I frowned as she stayed that way. I ran my gaze over her until I saw her name tag. Veronica Jones.

"Veronica? Are you okay? I vow to you, I mean you no harm. Your hands are busy and I figured having hair in your face must be frustrating. I'm truly sorry for touching you without permission. What can I do to help you?"

It was a small lie, but I wanted to make her feel safe, not freak her out even more by admitting how I'd been curious about how soft her skin was. She was having some sort of episode, and I wished like hell I knew who made her fear such a simple touch. I'd go after the fucker and make him pay for hurting this beautiful woman. I mentally shook my head. What the hell was I thinking? The last thing I needed right now was to get involved with a woman. What I needed was some down time where I could process everything that had happened. Wrap my head around that Josefina had been held and abused by Sabella for over a fucking decade thanks to me trying to fucking help her. The last thing this woman needed was my help. I barely held in my scoff. Just look at the damage I'd already managed to inflict on her.

She sucked in a deep breath and closed her eyes for a moment before she opened them. Without another word, she finished taping me up.

"Let me just grab the paperwork for you to sign, then you can be on your way."

Before I could say another word, she was gone. What the fuck?

I scrubbed my good hand over the un-singed side of my face, then I reached for my shirt and slowly put it back on. Probably for the best she was scared of me. I was in no shape to be in a relationship with any woman, let alone one who clearly had issues with men. Nope, if I got an itch my palm couldn't handle I'd take it up with one of the club whores that hung around the Charon MC clubhouse. Assuming I would be allowed to, anyway. I wasn't really part of the club, so I wasn't sure how many liberties I could take.

Veronica returned with my paperwork and by the look on her face, she had no intention of discussing what happened earlier. I decided to let it go and just followed her instructions to the letter. Before I knew it, I was discharged and walking out of the ER, back into the waiting room.

Mac and Nitro stood as I entered.

"How'd it go? Get the phone number of that nurse?"

I shook my head at Mac's question. "I wish, brother. Let's get outta here."

Nitro rubbed his chin as we made our way outside. "She was a strange one. Generally locals see the Charon MC colors and relax, but her first thought was that we were holding you against your will or something. It's the only reason she'd keep us from going back with you. Did you chat with her at all? If she's in some kind of trouble, we need to tell Scout and get Keys investigating it."

I shrugged a shoulder, not sure if I wanted to tell him my suspicions.

"Blade, man, we're not about poking our noses where they're not wanted, but after all the shit that's gone down over the past few years with women who've been new to town, we're paying more attention to the females here who might be in trouble now."

I didn't know much about what had gone down. It wasn't like Mac and I spoke all that often, and when we did, it wasn't to shoot the shit about life in general.

"She was fine until I stupidly touched her." Nitro and Mac both stopped walking and turned on me with matching glares that would take down a lesser man. I raised my hands in surrender. "Nothing like that! Damn, what do you think I am? She had a lock of hair hanging in her face and I tucked it behind her ear. I did it without thought. But she froze up and was cold toward me after she ignored my attempts to apologize."

We started walking again, both men no longer glaring but frowning.

Nitro was the first to speak. "I'll let Scout know. With that kinda reaction, there's a good chance she's been through some shit. Get her name? I didn't get a good read on her name tag."

"Veronica Jones."

"Maybe get to Donna, see what she knows about her."

I looked to Mac. "Who's Donna?"

"Keys' old lady. She works as a nurse here. Kinda surprised she didn't look after you. She normally jumps on any Charon cases."

Nitro nodded to Mac. "I don't think she's working the ER at the moment. And Blade's not wearing colors, so no one would have grabbed her for him."

Yep, I wasn't wearing a leather vest with a winged skull on the back so I wasn't one of them. I appreciated Mac giving me a safe place to heal up, but I wasn't sure how long I could take this "You're welcome, but hey, just remember you're not really one of us" thing. It got old fast. As I slid into the rear of the car, I decided I was going to grab a bottle of Maker's Mark from the bar then head up to my room for the rest of the day and night. I wasn't in the mood to smile and chat with a bunch of men who didn't know a fucking thing about me or what I was going through.

Blade

A knock on the door had me slowly waking up. Fuck. My brain felt like it was being jackhammered. In the past ten days, the only time I'd left my room here at the clubhouse was to get another bottle of Maker's. If I stayed drunk enough, I could get through the day without my thoughts being filled with Josefina. Unfortunately, it didn't seem to matter how much I consumed when it came to my nightmares. Even if I drank until I passed the fuck out, I still spent the night trapped in a horror show.

A knock sounded again. "Blade? You still breathin' in there?"

I rolled my eyes, then winced as pain flared through my poor, abused brain at Mac's words.

"I'm breathin'." *Barely.*

He opened the door I hadn't bothered to lock and barged in. His whole body shuddered before he put a hand over his mouth and nose.

"Fuck, man, it's rank in here."

He went over and opened the blinds, making me wince again as the light sent another dagger through my brain, then opened the window.

"C'mon, get your ass outta bed and in the shower. I'm taking you someplace. You got fifteen minutes to meet me downstairs or I'm coming back in here with a fucking hose to wash the stink off you."

With that, he spun and left my room, the breeze from the open window catching the door and slamming it behind him.

"Fuuuck."

Knowing Mac well enough to know he would really bring a damn hose up here to spray me with cold water, I dragged my ass to the edge of the bed. Forcing my body to sit up, I swung my legs over the side and with my head hung low, gave myself a few moments to adjust to being almost upright.

With a groan, I pushed up to my feet and stumbled over to the small bathroom that was attached to my room. I'd fallen into bed still wearing half my clothes, so it didn't take long for me to strip what was left off. Then I stood in front of the mirror and slowly peeled the dressings off my arm. Probably should have changed them a few days ago and I hoped like fuck the burns hadn't gotten infected or anything from my lack of care toward them over the past week.

Once the dressings were nothing more than a wad in the trash, I rotated my arm and looked at the healing wounds. Nothing looked like it was infected. The blisters were nearly all gone and the areas that had only been scorched rather than burned were almost back to my normal skin color. Thank fuck.

I turned on the water in the shower and made the temperature as cool as I could take it. Figuring, like sunburn, the last thing my burns needed was a hot spray of water.

Ten minutes later I was washed, dried and dressed. I'd not bothered putting a new dressing on my arm and had skipped my usual long sleeved shirt in favor of a black t-shirt that left my burns open to the air. *Let nature do its thing.* Veronica's sweet voice echoed around in my head, making me wince yet again. Both because my brain still felt like it was sloshing around inside my skull, and because I'd hurt her somehow with my touching her cheek and hair. Maybe I should drop back into the hospital just to check that she was okay and to apologize again…

Mac busting through my door once more had that thought vanishing from my mind as I noticed what he was carrying.

"You were seriously gonna throw a bucket of water at me?"

He shrugged as he headed to the bathroom to empty it out. "Scout wouldn't let me bring a hose up here. You ready to go?"

"I guess, but where are you taking me, exactly?"

He left the now empty bucket on the floor near the sink.

"You need to get away from these four walls, get some fresh air and talk to people."

I glared at him. "That told me exactly nothing. Where, Mac?"

He threw his hands up as he strode past me. "Where the fuck do you think I'm taking you? Home. I'm taking you to my house where you can see how Sparrow's doing and meet my old lady. Is that okay? Or are you gonna give me grief?"

I clenched my jaw against the curse I wanted to let out. I'd been surrounded by made men since I was fucking sixteen years old. I knew better than to trust *anyone*. Mac should have remembered that, he'd had enough time with those fuckers to have learned that lesson too.

"Could have led with that. You know why I'm as suspicious as I am."

The tension left Mac's body and he dropped his head down as he looked at the floor for a moment. When he lifted his gaze he caught mine and held it.

"If you decide to stay, to make a life here in Bridgewater, those days are over. The club is fucking loyal. Every man here has your back."

I shook my head. "They have *your* back. I ain't one of you."

"You can be, if you want it. Scout's all but offered it to you. It'll need to go to a vote in front of the club, but with everything you've done for us, I'm sure everyone will vote yes."

I turned and headed out the door. "It's too soon for me to be making any decisions for the long term. I still have no fucking clue of what fallout is gonna come my way from what we did in L.A."

Mac followed me down the stairs. "Keys is monitoring all the news sites and has calls into a few of his contacts over that way. He'll let you know if he hears anything."

I let the conversation drop, but considering I'd been their number one contact in L.A., I had no clue who the fuck Keys had over there. But unless they'd been in Antonio's inner circle, they'd be useless. And I highly doubted he had someone that close to the top. I knew each of those bastards and not one of them had any morals at all. I'd been living in a nest of vipers for decades. I'd been there so long that now I was out, I apparently didn't know how to live with normal people.

"How is Sparrow settling in?"

Mac's face lit up with pride. "She'd doing good, all things considered. She loves Cleo, and that girl has her big sister firmly wrapped around her little finger already."

That had me grinning. I'd yet to meet Mac's ten-month-old daughter, but I'd heard plenty about the little spitfire.

"She's gonna have you on your toes when she gets older."

Mac winced. "Yeah, we know. Let me tell you, I am not looking forward to that girl as a teenager."

I chuckled as I got into Mac's car. I didn't currently have a bike, but I'd ridden in the past. If I did decide to stay and give the club a go, one of the benefits would be the excuse to get another one. I'd missed the freedom I'd felt when I'd been out on the open road with the wind in my face.

43

Chapter 3

Blade

It was an hour later that I found myself sitting on Mac and Zara's back porch sipping iced tea—because Zara had declared my liver needed a break—and looking over their backyard and into the scrub that their placed backed onto.

Zara stood up and lifted Cleo up from where she was sitting playing with Sparrow. Mac had been right, the teenager was clearly completely besotted with her new baby sister.

"I'm going to go change Cleo and put her down for her nap."

"I'll help."

That was about as subtle as a sledgehammer. I rolled my eyes. I seriously doubted Zara needed help with their daughter. When they both went inside, Sparrow shifted from her spot on the ground to the seat next to mine.

"I wanted to thank you."

My hand was wrapped around the cold glass and I tapped my thumb against it as I glanced over at the teen.

"Thank me for what, darlin'?"

Been in town one fucking week and I was already calling girls darlin'. Texas was wearing off on me damn fast.

"For giving up your place here for me. For making them take me in."

I shook my head. "No need to thank me, Sparrow. I'm a grown-ass man, I don't need a family to fuss over me. And Mac would've brought you home with him no matter what I said. All I did was give him a push in the direction he was already heading."

She frowned down at her hands as she picked at her nails for a few moments, making me worry I'd offended her somehow with what I'd said. But fuck it all, I wasn't the hero in this story. Mac was the one who'd taken her into his home, Zara the one helping her adjust to her new life.

"You know, we all need family. There's enough room for us both."

My heart kicked in my chest at her innocent words. Unsure what to say, I lifted my glass to take another gulp of iced tea, wishing it was a different kind of amber liquid. After putting my drink back down, I cleared my throat and pretended like she hadn't said that last bit.

"I'm glad you're settling in here so well. You deserve it."

She frowned and ran her way too perceptive hazel gaze over my face. "Why'd you do it?"

"Do what?"

"Push Mac to bring me here. You could have just as easily pushed him to hand me over with the others. Was it because of that woman at the warehouse? The one who didn't make it."

With a sigh, I released my tight grip on the glass and slumped back into the chair, scrubbing my left hand over my face, being careful to avoid the still reddened parts on the right side. Guess Sparrow had overheard someone talking about Josefina. Since I got the impression she wasn't going to quit until I gave her something, I tried to decide what to tell her. How much to tell her. I figured after what she'd already been through, the whole truth wouldn't shock her too much, and really, what could it hurt? Might even make her appreciate what she had here a little more if she heard what could have happened.

"You sure you wanna hear all this? Might give you nightmares."

She rolled her eyes. "I already have those."

Leaning forward, I rested my elbows on my knees and looked straight into her eyes. "What you went through was bad, but it was nothing on what Josefina went through. Be sure you wanna know this shit, kid."

"I need to know. To make sense of why you, a stranger to me, helped me after my own flesh and blood sold me to those bastards."

I gave her a nod. Made sense. Huffing out a breath, I decided if she wanted it, she could have it.

"Two reasons I stepped up for you. Not only because of Josefina, but because of me. We're not so different, Sparrow. It wasn't my mom who sold me, but my dad. He owed protection money for his store that he didn't want to pay, or couldn't pay. Who knows? Anyhow, he cleared the debt by giving me to Sabella. I was sixteen. I didn't choose that life. Never would have if it had been up to me. But my old man threatened to hurt my mom and little brother if I didn't do what Sabella told me. My body was never raped, but my mind," I paused and tapped my temple, "those bastards fucked with my head in a big way. Tried everything they could to make me be like them. Dark and heartless."

Tears sat on her lashes and my breath caught for a moment.

"Don't cry for me, sweetheart. I ain't worth it."

She opened her mouth to say something but I shook my head, stopping her. Even after all she'd been through, the kid had a big heart. But I couldn't handle her turning it on me.

"I first met Josefina when I was twenty-one and she was sixteen. Thought it was a random meeting at the time but I learned later it was a set-up. Sabella had bought her from a Mexican cartel, who'd stolen her from her parents' farm. He'd left her drugged and abused on the street for me to find, to see what I'd do."

"He hoped you'd bring her in, right?"

I nodded. "Yeah, but I didn't." I had to pause to clear my throat against the lump that had formed there. "I took her home. Treated her like a sister. Let her get cleaned up, gave her clothes, food. Not that it mattered. Three months later I came home and she was gone. Sabella had come and taken what he deemed was his property. I went to him about her. It was the first time I'd gone up against him. I was so furious at him, I didn't think. Just barged straight into his office."

I paused to take another drink. "He had his men beat me, all the while telling me what he did to Josefina before he sold her to some other fucker who used her so hard she died." I stopped talking. I just couldn't say another damn word.

"He lied to you."

I nodded.

"Did you know she would be in that warehouse before you saw her?"

I nodded again. "A few hours before we stormed the warehouse, we found out that he'd lied. He'd kept her all those years as his personal toy. Until that day. That day he'd handed her over to his men, who had been wanting a piece of her for the last seventeen years. We were too late. She died in my arms."

I shook myself and stood, pacing across the porch.

"When I first saw you in that filthy room, you reminded me of her. They'd knocked you down but you were still ready to fight. Josefina had been like that when I'd first met her. Her clothes had been torn up, she was coming down off whatever drugs they'd given her, but she still put up a fight against Gino, the man I was with when we found her. Then, in the van, you were surrounded by big, tough men who you knew could cause harm yet you stood your ground—"

Her chuckle cut me short, and I spun to look at her.

"I was hardly brave, Blade. I was desperate and happy to beg for what I needed. I knew if I was given to the authorities I'd end up back with my mother, who'd just sell me all over again. Anything was better than that."

"What about your father?"

I wondered if she even knew who he was. With a wince, she shrugged a shoulder. "Never met him. Mom told me he'd rather see me dead than have me in his presence, so I'm happy to never go down that road."

Fuck, she'd struck out in the parent department big time.

"I'm sorry, Sparrow. I at least had my mom. She loved me as much as she could while being under my dad's thumb."

"What happened to her and your brother?"

I smiled, for probably the first time in a week. "They're fine. Not long after everything went down with Josefina, I got new identities for them and helped them sneak out of my father's house. They're nowhere near California and have lived peaceful lives for a long time. I check in with them a couple of times a year."

"It must be hard to not see them. You should bring them here. They'd be safe here."

I chuckled. "I like that you have so much faith in the Charons, honey, but they're happy where they are. I wouldn't want to uproot them and make them start over again. It wouldn't be fair."

"I'd suggest you could go to them, but I get the feeling you don't want to leave here. I know Mac doesn't want you to."

I gave her a raised eyebrow. "You see too much, kid."

She shrugged her shoulders and took a sip of her own iced tea as we both fell into a comfortable silence, staring out at the trees and shit that surrounded the yard. It was strange that I somehow felt lighter for having shared what I had with Sparrow. I just hoped I hadn't given the kid a whole slew of new nightmares to suffer though.

Mac strode out a few minutes later and from the look on his face, I suspected he'd been inside eavesdropping on our conversation. Not that I blamed him. He'd taken Sparrow in fully and was being a protective father for her.

That got me thinking about how Mac had been treating me since I got burned.

"Mac, you know I didn't do that shit on purpose, right? The can slipped in my grip and splashed every-fucking-where. After I lit the room up, a spark came my way and I'd forgotten that I was soaked in gas when I tried to bat it away from me. I've never once been suicidal in my life."

He gave me a nod. "I was worried that shit with your girl had broken you." He heaved out a heavy sigh. "How about we hit Styx tonight? Change of scenery from the clubhouse."

I huffed out a laugh. "Yeah, brother, the club-owned bar is gonna be a real change of pace from the bar in the clubhouse."

Only change I could see going in was that I'd be paying for my drinks while they'd been free at the clubhouse, but whatever. If Mac wanted to head out, I'd join him. It probably was time I got out and started interacting with people in the real world anyhow. Making decisions about what I wanted to do with the rest of my life now that I wasn't bound to Antonio.

Veronica

In the ten days since I'd treated Mr. Jared Walker, I hadn't been able to shake him from my mind. It was insane. More than once, he'd filled my dreams, which I will admit, was a welcome relief from the nightmares that usually filled my nights. But it still had me on edge. I'd never actually been with a lover of my own choosing, never wanted to. After escaping, my whole world had been solely about staying hidden and surviving. In my experience, sex was just something a man forced upon a woman when he wanted it.

My body convulsed as a vision of my uncle looming over me filled my mind. Bile rose up my throat and I rushed to the bathroom, barely making it in time before I emptied my stomach. By the time I washed my face and stared in the mirror at my pale reflection, I wondered if going out tonight was a bad idea. Maybe I should stay in.

The timer on my phone chimed, letting me know I only had ten minutes before the girls would be here to pick me up. I couldn't cancel. If I did, there'd be even more questions that I didn't want to answer. In the seven years I'd been in Bridgewater, I'd made a few friends among the staff at the hospital, but I'd never let anyone all the way in. My secrets stayed with me, locked away.

With a huff, I dried my face and set about quickly fixing my makeup, hoping by the time the others got here, they wouldn't notice I'd been sick. It wasn't often a flashback got to me enough to make me physically ill, but I'd been preoccupied with thoughts of Jared and had not been paying attention to where my mind was heading until it was too late.

"Stop it."

Blowing out a breath, I forced my thoughts away from the past. Nothing good would ever come from it. By the time a horn honked out the front, I was as ready as I was going to be. Snatching up my purse, I headed out my front door, carefully locking things up before heading toward the little hatchback waiting for me.

Pulling open the rear door, I slid in and couldn't help but smile. Sophie and Laura both beamed big grins at me.

"You ready for some biker eye candy, girl?"

Laura scoffed at Sophie's question. "Girlfriend's been hankering for a more classy type of candy than biker."

Naturally, they'd both caught wind of my treating Jared and had teased me about it ever since.

"I doubt I'll ever see him again. He was just another patient."

That thought had me torn. It was probably for the best. My life didn't have room in it for a romantic entanglement, but on the other hand, when I'd been close to him, I'd felt alive. Something about his striking blue eyes drew me in and I was helpless to stop it. Well, until he touched me. Then I'd behaved like a frightened mouse. I'm sure if I did see him again, he'd either laugh at the memory, or not remember me at all.

Sophie wriggled her eyebrows in the rear-view mirror at me as she pulled up into the parking lot of Styx.

"Well, let's see if we can find you something down and dirty to distract you tonight."

Since it was only a little past eight on a Thursday night, the parking lot was about half full, and that included a very nice lineup of Harleys that I took my time walking past. So much chrome to keep clean and polished. I couldn't help but wonder if these men would treat a woman like they treated their bikes? Or were all men more like my uncle?

Squeezing my eyes closed for a moment, I forced those thoughts away. Not tonight. I wasn't going to allow myself to fall down that hole tonight.

When an arm hooked behind mine, my eyes flipped open to see Sophie's worried face.

"Babe, you know we're just joking, right? We're gonna go in, sit at our usual table, have a few drinks and watch all the untouchable bikers for a few hours before we all head home again. No pressure to even talk to one of them."

I patted her hand. She was a good friend and I wished I wasn't so messed up. Wished I could find a way to explain why I was the way I was, without revealing the reason why. She knew something had happened to me. She and Laura both had nailed that down early on in our friendship, but I'd never offered up the information and thankfully, they'd never pushed me for it.

"I'm good. Just needed a moment. Hey, how long do you think those guys have to spend polishing their bikes? Some of them have a serious amount of chrome on them."

Laura came and took Sophie's other arm. "I think they're compensating for something. Like the shinier the bike, the smaller the—" She winked at us without finishing her sentence before we broke apart and went through the door into the dimly lit interior of the bar.

I liked coming into Styx, it held a lot of charm. And it didn't try to pretend to be something it wasn't. So many bars tried to make themselves into night clubs, but not Styx. The music was old-school rock and it wasn't turned up to a level that would leave your ears bleeding. The lighting was dim, but not so dark you couldn't see the person next to you. The bar and tables were made out of polished timber and the chairs and stools were all sturdy enough to hold the weight of the largest of bikers. The clientele suited me too. They were rough and real. No fancy businessmen in suits and ties came here. The other thing I loved, was everyone left you alone. The three of us came in at least a couple times a month and sat at our table to watch those around us and never once had anyone bothered us.

Following our usual routine, we went to the bar, ordered drinks then made our way to our table, which, thankfully was empty. Once I slid onto the seat, I put my purse in the center of the table. Sophie and Laura did the same thing. Then, after sucking down the first icy-cold mouthful of my gin and tonic, I took in the scenery for the first time.

Styx was one of the few places I didn't scope out the moment I entered. From the first time I'd come in, I'd felt safe here. It also helped that I knew nothing on this earth could entice my upper-class uncle to come in here for any reason.

So that's how I ended up with a mouthful of liquid when I saw him. The shock of seeing those striking blue irises staring straight at me had my breath catching. Then, because I hadn't swallowed the mouthful of my drink I'd taken, I half choked on it. Grabbing a napkin, I tried to not attract too much attention but it was getting a little late for that. Laura was thumping my back and Sophie was nearly peeing herself with laughter. My eyes were blurry from unshed tears and my sinuses were stinging from being doused in alcohol.

Finally, I stopped coughing and could take a damn breath.

"Here, darlin', drink some water." Nitro, the tall biker who was manning the bar more often than not when we came in, had come over, setting down a tall glass of ice water in front of me. I could feel the heat in my cheeks and knew I must look a hot mess. My eyes most likely were all red from the tears, my cheeks pink with embarrassment. I hoped that my mascara held and I didn't also have raccoon eyes going on to top off my look.

After a couple mouthfuls of water I cleared my throat. "Thanks. Turns out breathing liquid doesn't end well."

Once he was convinced I was going to be okay, he chuckled at my words before he turned and returned to his place behind the bar.

"Oh, hell, that was so damn embarrassing. I'm just gonna go into the bathroom and see what the damage is."

Laura and Sophie were both trying—poorly—to contain their laughter as those around us got back to what they'd been doing before I put on a show. I shook my head at them as I stood, grabbed my purse and headed for the bathroom.

Thanks to my mascara living up to its promise of being tear-proof, it didn't take me long to wipe my eyes—carefully, because I only had so much faith in that waterproof mascara—and be on my way back out to my girls.

"Oh."

He was there waiting, casually leaning against the wall opposite the bathroom door. At my gasp, his gaze snapped up and caught mine. My heart started racing as he tilted his head and kept looking at me.

"You okay?"

I cleared my throat. "Uh, yeah. Accidentally inhaled some of my drink. Not my finest moment."

His lips quirked up but the smile didn't hold.

"I wanted to apologize for last week at the hospital. I didn't mean to freak you out. Not sure why I even did it, to be honest."

As much as I was impressed he even remembered me, I didn't want him feeling guilty over something that should have been a non-issue.

"Listen, Jared—"

"It's Blade."

I frowned. "Huh?"

"My name. It's Blade. No one calls me Jared anymore."

"Oh, ah, okay. Well, Blade, it wasn't your fault. I, ah, I have some history that makes me a little more skittish than your average woman. I didn't mean to react like I did and I'm sorry it's had you worrying about me. Really, I'm fine."

He nodded. "I'll believe you if you let me take you out on a date so I can apologize properly."

My mind spun. A date? I'd basically just admitted I was a nut job and he wanted to what? Date me?

"Are you mad?"

He chuckled, the deep sound vibrating down my spine. "I've been called worse. So, will you let me take you out? We can meet somewhere, if you'd prefer. Keep it all in public and safe."

I shook my head. "I don't date."

His forehead crinkled. "What the hell do you mean you don't date? You're beautiful and young. How the fuck don't you date? I would have thought you'd be beating men off with a stick."

He was stubborn. I barely knew this man. *And you won't, if you don't give him a chance.* Apparently my subconscious was lonely. Or horny. Maybe both. He'd offered to meet me somewhere public. Maybe if we kept it to daylight hours, it might work. He wouldn't try anything handsy if we were in public in the day time, surely?

"Okay, no date. How about coffee, then? You working Saturday?"

I couldn't hold in my smile at this man's persistence. It seemed he really wanted to see me again. I sincerely hoped I wouldn't regret this…

"Okay. Ten-thirty, Marie's Cafe, this Saturday."

He gave me a grin and a nod, but didn't reach for me. "Thank you, baby. You won't regret it."

I winced at the endearment I hated with a passion. "Please don't call me that."

He cocked his head. "You mean all endearments or just baby?"

"Just that one. I'm born and bred Texan, so trust me, I'm used to endearments in general. It's just that one I don't like."

He gave me another nod. "I'll need to think of something else then, something special." He held me with his gaze as he stood away from the wall and moved slowly closer to me. My breath caught in my throat as my heart pounded against my ribs. My gaze dropped to his lips, which were surrounded by a short beard. They looked soft. Was he going to kiss me? Did I want him to? I was stuck. I had no clue what to do, what I wanted. With a whimper I bit at my lower lip and lifted my gaze back to his. Those striking blue irises of his caught my full attention and calmed my mind.

When he got too close for me to stay focused on, my eyes slid shut, waiting for him to do whatever it was he was going to. The soft hair of his beard tickled my skin a moment before his lips, which were as soft as they looked, pressed a gentle kiss to the side of my temple.

"Till Saturday, my little dove."

Be still my heart.

Blade

Walking away from Veronica last night was one of the hardest things I'd ever done. The woman was as sweet as she was skittish. There was definitely something going on under the surface with her. I wasn't sure if she was on the run and hiding, or if it was something simpler like her last boyfriend being a fucking bastard to her. Either way, I wanted to find out more, if I could, before I met her tomorrow at Marie's Cafe.

That was why I was up earlier than usual this morning and jogging down the stairs to the lower level of the clubhouse. I'd spoken with Keys last night before leaving Styx and he'd told me to meet him in his office at ten. When I got to his office, I knocked on the open door before I made my way in. He was behind his desk, intently staring at the laptop screen in front of him.

"Hey, Keys."

He tapped away for a few more seconds before he stopped and switched his focus to me.

"How serious are you about this girl?"

I took a seat and leaned back before answering him. "Not sure. Only met her twice. We have some killer chemistry but she's skittish as hell. My instincts say there's something deeper going on with her." I shrugged a shoulder. "Mac mentioned your club likes to keep tabs on women who might be running from something, so even if she and I don't pan out, I think it's something worth checking into."

Keys nodded. "Yeah, after everything that went down with Zara, Mercedes, and a few of the other women around town, we started thinking it would be a good idea for us to be a little more proactive in sensing these threats before they hit us." He paused for a minute, looking to his screen again and hitting a few keys.

"My old lady, Donna, is a nurse up at the hospital. I asked her about your Veronica but she hasn't had much to do with her. Guess the younger ones do their own thing outside of work. She did say that she's never seen her cause trouble and she's always done a good job whenever

Donna's worked with her. So with that being a dead end, I headed to the web."

He stopped and gave me a raised eyebrow which just frustrated the fuck out of me.

"And? What have you found?"

"Turns out, you're right. Veronica Jones ain't her real name. Not sure what her real one is just yet, but the Veronica identity was a budget job. Easy to pick it's fake with a little digging. However, it's taking me a little longer to dig up her real identity. When are you seeing her again?"

"I'm meeting her at Marie's Cafe tomorrow morning. Why?"

"Because Scout and I might come crash your date. We need to know what she's running from and if it's likely to come at us."

Panic had my heart skipping a beat as I shook my head. "She'll run if you do that. She's skittish as hell. I'm not even sure she'll actually turn up tomorrow. I was a little shocked she agreed to it, to be honest."

Keys glared my way. "How, exactly, did you get to the point of asking her out then, if she's that damn skittish?"

I frowned at him. "You asking how we met?"

"More than that. I can figure out that you met at the hospital, I'm more interested in what happened after that first meeting."

I took the man in. He was probably in his early to mid-sixties and had lived life hard. He had a glint in his eye that had me certain he'd done time in the military at some point. From Mac, I knew Keys was the club's IT guy. The one who, if he didn't already know something, knew exactly how to find it out.

I liked Veronica. There was something about the woman that drew me in and had me dreaming of more. Something I'd not even considered since the day my dad handed my ass over to Sabella. There was a fragility I sensed beneath her surface that I wanted to protect, and fresh on the reality of how poorly I'd protected Josefina, I decided to trust Keys with her.

"She was the one who saw me to redress my burns at the hospital. All was going well, nice, casual chatting while she did her thing. Then without fucking thinking, I reached out to tuck a lock of her hair behind her ear. My fingers grazed her cheek and she shut right down. Took a few minutes, but she came back to reality and finished patching me up, but was all professional about it. The friendly banter from earlier had vanished. I tried to apologize but I doubt she heard me since she was still lost in thought at the time. Then she was done and gone before I could get the words out to try again."

"So your hiding out in your room wasn't just over the woman in L.A. but this one too? Damn, man, you're working on cornering the market on guilt, aren't you? You sure you didn't just startle her?"

"Yeah, seems I got a talent. And no, she got lost in her head for a few minutes. Her skin paled—hell, I thought she was gonna pass out on me for a little bit. Once I left the hospital, I figured I wouldn't see her again, not since my burns were healing up fine. Then yesterday, I guess Mac got sick of me wallowing around upstairs and he dragged me over to his place, then later over to Styx. No one was more shocked then me when she came strolling in with two friends." I smiled as I remembered what happened next. "She and her girls went to the bar, got drinks then settled in at one of the rear tables. When she looked up and caught me staring at her, she choked on her drink."

Keys chuckled. "Heard about that. Didn't realize it was your chick. Okay, so she had a reaction to seeing your ugly mug. What'd you do about it?"

"When she went to the bathroom I waited in the hallway for her. When she came out, she hadn't expected to see me there, but she wasn't scared, exactly. I kept my place by the wall and we chatted. Apologized again, she told me it wasn't my fault. Then, when I asked her on a date, she froze up, got ready to panic. So I backtracked, told her we'd start small. Daytime, in public. In the end, she suggested we have coffee at Marie's tomorrow morning. But, Keys, I'm serious. That woman is constantly on the verge of running. You and Scout come in and she'll freak the fuck out and bolt on me."

Keys shrugged. "Okay. We'll leave you to it for now. But see if you can find out where she's from, or where she was born, at least. Anything to give me a start on looking for her real ID. The chances anything's gonna come for her are slim. She's been in town for seven years already and nothing's found her yet. That said, you notice anyone following her or anything even remotely suspicious, you need to come tell us."

I went to stand. "Easy enough. That all you need me for?"

He nodded. "Yep. What's your plan for the rest of the day?"

That had me grinning. "Figured I might go up to Kingwood and do a little shopping."

Keys' eyes lit up like a damn Christmas tree at the mention of the town with the closest Harley dealership. "That right? You ridden before?"

"Yeah, used to have a Heritage Classic, but Sabella made me get rid of it. Some shit about it not befitting his organization." I held my arm out and flexed my wrist, the tug on my healing burns wasn't too bad now. "Think I've healed up enough to ride without too much trouble."

"Yeah, good deal. Who's going with you up there?"

"Mac and Sparrow."

His expression softened at the teen's name. "That kid's something else, isn't she? Only met her real quick the other day but she seems to be settling in with Mac and his crew well."

"Yeah, she's a fighter, for sure. It'll take her while to adjust to her new reality fully, I'm sure. But she's definitely made a good start. I just hope she doesn't try to talk me into getting a fucking purple bike or some shit."

Keys barked out a laugh. "I'm sure she'll try it. Good luck, man and let me know when you get back so I can come check it out."

I headed to the door chuckling. "You just wanna see if I do give in to whatever the hell Sparrow will try to talk me into."

"Well, yeah, that too."

As I headed down the hall toward the main bar, my mind went back to Veronica. What the hell had happened to her that she'd needed a new identity? It was going to be hard to not ask her tomorrow, to pretend like I didn't know information about her that she hadn't told me herself. Especially when it was so fucking important. I couldn't keep her safe if I didn't know everything.

Chapter 4

Veronica

At ten-thirty-five I rushed through the door to Marie's Cafe, hoping like hell Jared, er, I mean Blade hadn't been waiting for too long. Or even worse, had thought I'd stood him up and had left. I skidded to a halt when I saw he was up at the counter, by the big coffee machine, chatting with a beautiful woman with a mane of strawberry blonde hair standing behind the machine. Jealousy ripped through me like a knife and stole my breath. I took a step back, intending on going back out and getting far away from Blade and this cafe.

"Hey, Veronica! You made it."

My feet wouldn't move as he prowled over toward me. The way that man's hips rolled when he walked was sigh-worthy. But, wait, I was mad at him. I'd caught him flirting with another woman. Not that we were like a thing or anything… Before I could convince my feet to take me back outside, he was standing in front of me, wrapping one arm around my waist and pulling me closer to him. Out of reflex, I raised my palms, which landed against his hard, toned pecs. The thin button-down shirt he wore did nothing to stop the heat coming off him from radiating through to my palms.

"Thought you'd stood me up for a minute there, darlin'. Thought I was gonna have to come find you."

I could hear the humor in his voice, but the words still made me shudder. I didn't need anyone else out there trying to find me.

"Just running a little late, that's all." I nodded to the counter. "You know her?"

I caught his smirk a moment before he leaned in and, just like Thursday night, pressed a gentle kiss to the side of my temple.

"Zara is Mac's old lady. It's cute you're jealous, though."

He pulled away but kept his hand on my lower back and guided me over to a table.

"I am not jealous. And what the hell do you mean, old lady?"

The woman looked about my age, certainly not old.

Like a total gentleman, he pulled the chair out for me, before he moved to sit himself.

"Sure, little dove, you're not jealous at all when you came racing in here to see me, only to find me chatting with another woman. You weren't trying to backpedal outta here, hoping I didn't see you. And an old lady is what bikers call their woman. Not necessarily their wife, although I do believe Mac and Zara are legally married."

Before I could think of something to say back, the woman in question was beside our table.

"Hi, I'm Zara. It's lovely to meet you. You're a nurse at the hospital, right? I think I've seen you up there. Do you know Donna? She's with one of the other brothers."

The woman was so warm and friendly, I found myself smiling and introducing myself before I knew what I was doing.

"Hi, um, yeah I'm a nurse, and I've worked with Donna before, but I don't know her well. I'm Veronica."

Zara gave me a huge smile. "Ah, well, keep hanging out with Blade and I'm sure you'll spend more time with her around the clubhouse and get to know her better. She really is a lovely woman. Anyhow, let me take your order and I'll let you get back to chatting."

Her immediate assumption that Blade and I were going to continue to see each other had me shocked mute for a minute.

"An espresso, no cream, no sugar. Thanks, Zara. Veronica?"

I mentally shook myself. "Ah, chai latte, thanks."

"Any pie? We've got blueberry or apple."

"Sure, apple would be great."

"Make that two."

Zara headed back to the counter, leaving me alone with Blade again.

"The girls at work rave about the pie here. Apparently Marie has some sort of gift."

"You've never come here before to try it for yourself?"

I shook my head. "I don't go out much, really."

He cocked his eyebrow and smirked at me. "What sent you out to Styx then?"

I rolled my eyes. "I said I don't go out much, not that I never go out."

"I'm just wondering what Styx has that draws you out when rumors of the best pie around hasn't enticed you to come in here."

Zara came up and set our drinks in front of us, then two plates, each with a large slice of apple pie.

"Think about it, Blade. Eye candy. All you biker boys hang out down at Styx. Women aren't ruled by the stomach, like you men. Although, once you try this pie, I'm sure you'll be back for more."

With a wink my direction, she slipped away, leaving me sitting there ready to die of embarrassment. My cheeks were so hot I was sure they were bright red. His deep, rumbly chuckle did not help matters.

"My little dove wanted something pretty to look at, huh? That why you and your girls go out to Styx?"

I shrugged as I forked up a piece of pie and shoved it into my mouth so I couldn't speak. Then I moaned. Damn, that pie really was good.

Blade chuckled before taking a mouthful of his own slice.

"Hmm, that is a damn good pie."

Everything out of his mouth sounded dirty, like he was making sexual innuendos out of everything. Or maybe I was just so desperate, it was me who was hearing it rather than him putting it out there.

I hadn't taken a lover since I'd run away. Hadn't wanted to. Until now. There was something about Blade that was getting to me. Turning on parts of me that I'd thought I'd turned off for good. I wasn't sure how I felt about it all. I mean, I hadn't really consciously decided that I'd be single forever, but I'd assumed that would be the case. Even if I was brave enough to try to sleep with

Blade, what would happen when he tried to touch me? I mean, I'd freaked the fuck out when he'd barely touched my cheek. What the fuck would happen if he tried to get me naked?

"Wherever you just went, don't."

His rough voice brought me out of my thoughts and I looked up from my plate into his piercing blue eyes.

"Whatever happened to you in the past? It's over. I won't ever hurt you, and I sure as hell won't let anyone else hurt you, either."

"You can't know that. Can't promise that."

He leaned in toward me. "Let me tell you a little about myself, little dove. At sixteen, my father sold me to the mob. For the past twenty-two years, I've been living among the vilest of men, doing what I had to in order to survive. Two weeks ago, I got out. While I have zero intentions of ever going back to that life, the skills it taught me will never leave me, and I have no problem using every last one of them to keep you safe. Understand?"

I froze under his intensity. I was totally unprepared for how to deal with this man.

"I, ah, no, I don't understand. You don't know me—"

"So tell me about you. What I know so far has me wanting more. Tell me the rest of your secrets, Veronica. They're all safe with me, I promise."

Panic shook me to my core. Did he already know? Had my uncle sent him?

"Where did you live? When you were in the mob?"

"Los Angeles. Why? Is that who hurt you? Someone with connections? Veronica, I have no connections to that life anymore. I got out and burned all the bridges I had in order to leave. I'm here in town because I've known Mac a long time and he offered me a place to stay while I heal and decide what I want for the rest of my life. I'm not a threat to you, I promise."

I began to feel lightheaded. This was all too much. I had no idea if I could believe him. I had no one I could trust to talk to about him, either. I'd kept myself so damn isolated, I had no one to go to. Sure, Sophie and Laura were friends, but neither of them even knew that Veronica wasn't my real name.

I had to get away. I couldn't do this.

I shoved my chair out and stood in a rush.

"I can't. I gotta go."

I nearly tripped over the chair leg as I turned but I kept going, rushing to the door, then through it. Ignoring Blade calling out my name. Struggling to draw in enough air, I stumbled out to the parking lot. Desperate to get away, I didn't pay attention like I normally did. Didn't take in the area for threats. Just went directly to my car. A horn blasting had me jolting a moment before a strong arm wrapped around my waist and hauled me back against a solid chest.

A dark green sedan drove past, the driver shaking his head at me as a sob broke free. I knew who held me. Blade's scent had enveloped me the moment he'd grabbed me.

"What the fuck, Veronica? You could've been killed!"

Before I could track what was happening, he had my back up against the rear wall of the cafe with his big, hard body stopping me from going anywhere. Tears blurred my eyes as I looked up into his furious, icy gaze. The second our gazes clashed, his softened, he lifted his hand, and ran his knuckles down my cheek.

"Don't ever be scared of me, Veronica." He leaned in and pressed another gentle kiss to my temple, melting me inside. But he didn't stop there. Nope, he continued pressing them down the side of my face, over my cheek, to the edge of my mouth. "You gonna let me kiss you? I swear you just took ten years off my life with that little stunt. I need you to calm me down. I need a taste of you."

I knew I should say no, should push him away. I raised my hands and fisted them in the front of his shirt. I should push. But I didn't. I pulled him in closer, turned my head slightly and pressed my lips against his, hoping he'd take control. I'd never been kissed, had no clue how to do it. But suddenly, I wanted it with Blade. I wanted to see where this fire he'd started within me would lead. Maybe it was strong enough, hot enough, to burn away those old memories and give me some new ones I could cherish.

Blade

My heart was still pounding at how close she'd come to getting clipped by that car. Adrenaline was racing through my system, demanding an outlet. Since I had her pinned between me and a wall, she was my first choice. Her sweet scent filled my head, making me fucking dizzy. But I didn't want to push her too hard, scare her off. I'd spilled out my demand for her to let me kiss her before I'd fully thought it through. She was so fucking skittish. If I pushed too hard too fast, she'd bolt for sure.

Thankfully my words hadn't sent her running. Instead she took two fistfuls of my shirt and pulled me to her, turning her head to press her lips to mine. The moment our mouths connected, my brain short-circuited. With a growl, I cupped her face between my palms and tilted her head where I needed her to be so I could get full access to her lush little mouth. Then I laid my lips over hers and made her mine. A swipe of my tongue over her lower lip had her gasping and gave me the access I needed to dance my tongue with hers.

Her grip on my shirt tightened as she moaned into the kiss.

"Yo, Blade! This ain't the clubhouse, mate!"

Taz's smartass Aussie accent floated across the parking lot, breaking the moment.

I gave her one more light kiss before pulling away, stroking my thumbs over her cheeks as I kept my gaze locked on her glassy eyes. Slowly, her breathing calmed and she blinked her eyes clear. She ran the tip of her tongue over her lower lip and my already hard cock jerked against the fly of my pants in demand.

"What was that?"

"Me kissing you."

She swallowed, dropping her gaze away from mine. "Is it—" She cleared her throat and a blush colored her cheeks. "Is it always like that?"

That stopped me short. Was she asking what I thought she was?

"Look at me." I waited for her to lift her gaze before I continued. "You've never been kissed before, little dove?"

She shook her head against my palms that still cupped her face between them.

In a low, soft growl, I asked her the more important question. "Are you a virgin?"

I'd never been with a virgin, but something about being the only one to have this woman was doing it for me. Until her eyes widened in panic.

"No, of course not. I'm thirty-two years old, for crying out loud."

She tried to break away from my grip, but I sensed the falseness to her little rant just now. Oh, I was certain it was the truth, but the reason behind it had nothing to do with how old she was. How the fuck does a woman lose her virginity while never having been kissed? The conclusion my brain drew had rage flowing in my veins.

"Who hurt you? Tell me his name and I'll make sure he never gets near you again."

Her face paled as her eyes went wide. She held herself stiff for a moment, twisting her fists against my chest, then she seemed to deflate before me, tears filling her eyes.

"It's not your concern—"

I cut her off by slamming my palms against the wall on either side of her shoulders, ignoring the way the rough brick cut into my skin.

"Bullshit! You are my concern, Veronica. I will keep you protected, but it'll be fucking hard if my hands are tied behind my back. Tell me the information I need to make sure you stay safe."

"Blade, I've been living here for seven years and haven't seen or heard from him. I'm safe here. You don't need to do anything."

So she had been hurt. Fuck it all. I wanted blood on her behalf. Rage and fury held me motionless as she shifted her hands, releasing my shirt then reaching up to cup my face like I'd done to her earlier. She stroked her fingers through my short beard for a few moments and I closed my eyes at the feel of her soft hands on me. My imagination took the sensation and ran with it, picturing how it would feel to be naked before her, with her hands exploring my bare flesh, wrapping around my cock and stroking me.

Her lips pressing a soft kiss to the corner of my mouth had my mind back in the moment, and I opened my eyes in time to see her brush a tear away before she ducked under my arm and strode away from me.

I watched her go, torn about whether to chase her or not. Fuck it. I jogged after her, reaching her as she unlocked her car and opened the door.

"Wait! Veronica, don't leave like this. We need to talk about it."

With a huff, she turned on me. "Talk about what, Blade? That someone hurt me? Yeah, he did. But it's over and done with. I don't want to revisit it."

"Don't make me go looking for information, little dove. I'll do it because I need to know how to keep you safe, but I'd prefer you just tell me."

I winced when fear, clear as day, crossed her features. "You wouldn't dare! Do not go digging, Blade. You have no right. Leave my past the hell alone." She shook her head. "Leave *me* the hell alone."

"You don't mean that. You wouldn't have kissed me like you did if you really wanted me to leave you be. I'll follow you home, then we can talk in private."

I didn't give her a choice, just turned from her and strode over to my new bike. The black and chrome 2002 Fat Boy had been well cared for and I knew it was destined to be mine when I'd seen it earlier. I was extra grateful I now had a bike when she took off out of the lot, clearly trying to leave me behind. Fuck, I hoped she didn't call the cops on me for this, but I couldn't leave her alone after what just happened. I'd brought shit up from her past and no matter what she said, she'd be thinking about it now. That was my fault and I wanted to be there to comfort her. I also wanted to get to the bottom of what had happened to her, so I could make it all better for her.

With the taste of her kiss still on my lips, I twisted the throttle and followed her down the road. I was not going to let my girl get away that easily.

Veronica

No, no, no. This wasn't happening.

How the hell had I gone from flying so high to crashing so hard? I smacked my hands against my steering wheel as I glanced in the rear-view mirror to see a bike gaining on me. I knew I wouldn't be able to outrun him. As he drew closer, I could see the firm set of his jaw. He wasn't going to let this slide. I was going to have to tell him something. That, or call the cops on his ass. I shook my head. I wouldn't do that. In a way, it was nice to have someone care. Hopefully it didn't cost him what it had cost my parents.

I'm not sure how young I was when my uncle first started grooming me. I couldn't remember a time when he hadn't taken an unhealthy interest in me. The older I got, the further he pushed his seduction with me. By the time my parents figured out he was doing things that he shouldn't, I was in my early teens

They'd been devastated when I'd confessed how long he'd been doing things to me. But my uncle was the mayor, and not a clean and upstanding one. There was no way to make him pay through the legal system. So, my parents did what they could. They sent me away to boarding school.

I'd gotten six months of peace before my parents paid the price for taking me away from him. He killed them. Oh, sure, it was on the record as a tragic car accident where my dad lost control of their car and it went over a cliff. I never did believe that story. But none of that changed the fact in the aftermath of their deaths, my custody was handed over to the only remaining relative. My uncle. Who'd promptly pulled me from the boarding school and brought me home.

A full body shudder ran through me as I pulled up in front of my little house. The memories were crowding in on me, too many to force them all away. I didn't want this. Any of it. I hadn't wanted it back then, and I sure as fuck didn't want to relive it now. I sure as hell didn't want Blade to run off after my uncle and get himself hurt, or killed. When the loud rumble of his bike cut off, the air was unnaturally quiet. But I couldn't move. Couldn't peel my fingers away from the steering wheel to hit the garage door opener so I could put my car away. When my door opened, letting the cool outside air wash over me, I jerked against the seat but still I couldn't release my tight grip.

"Fuck, ba— Veronica."

He remembered I didn't like being called baby. Couldn't stand it. I was grateful he'd listened when I'd mentioned it the other day. Without moving, I watched as he turned the engine off and pulled the keys from the ignition, then gently pried my hands from the wheel, using his grip on them to pull me up and out of the car. Once standing, he wrapped his uninjured arm around my waist, pulling me in tightly against him as he closed my door and locked it. I normally put it in the garage but I'd worry about that later. I nuzzled my nose in against his chest, inhaling his scent. My head felt strange, like I couldn't quite grab the thoughts that were passing me by. But at least the memories were starting to fade away, for the moment.

"C'mon, gorgeous."

He scooped my trembling body up in his arms and I had the brief worry he was hurting his burns by carrying me, but before I could voice anything, the thought floated away. I kept my face pressed against him as he started moving. The next thing I knew, I was sitting in his lap on my couch, his touch gentle on my face and hair. He'd pulled my throw blanket over me and I was cozy and warm, curled up against his strong chest.

The comparison to how my uncle would hold me had me tensing for a moment, but before I completely lost my damn mind, I focused on the differences. Blade's hands were nowhere near the junction of my thighs or my boobs. He was stroking my hair and cheek gently. He hadn't removed any of my clothes, he'd only taken off my shoes before he'd pulled a blanket over me.

Blade was not my uncle.

He was not there to hurt me. *Hopefully.*

Taking a deep breath, I spread my fingers out over his chest, but I wanted more contact. Needed to be closer. Carefully, I slipped three buttons through their holes then slid my hand inside, my palm sliding over the smooth, warm skin of his pectoral muscle. Pressing it flat, I sighed at the feel of his heart thumping against my palm.

"You back with me, Veronica?"

"Hmm. How long was I out?"

"Not sure. Ten minutes or so. Scared the hell outta me, sweetheart. I was getting ready to call Keys to get Donna over here. That happen often?"

"I'm not even sure what that was…"

He reached under the blanket and flicked open the rest of his buttons. I lifted myself up for a moment as he leaned forward and shrugged out of it. "This okay?"

"Yeah, more than okay."

I snuggled back against him, loving how his warm skin felt against my cheek. How would it feel to be completely naked with him? I mentally shook my head. Nope, I wasn't going to push this there. Baby steps, I needed to take this thing in tiny, little, baby steps so I didn't freak out again.

"Good. I like having you in my arms, pressed against me. Close your eyes and get some rest, little dove. I've got you covered. Just forget about whatever the fuck I triggered. You're safe with me."

On some level I knew I was being stupidly naive for believing this man, but I was so damn tired and it felt so nice to be held by him. Felt good to have his muscular body surrounding mine, caging me in with a sensation of safety rather than danger. With a deep sigh, I once more nuzzled in against him and closed my eyes, letting myself go.

Chapter 5

Blade

What a fucking week.

After a long, sleepless night on Veronica's couch holding her while she slept like the dead against my bare chest, I'd hauled my ass back to the clubhouse to discover Bash's—one of the prospects—mother had passed away. Man was understandably a mess and everyone was focused on getting him through the week. I didn't know him well enough to know what was going on in his head, but with how withdrawn he'd been, it didn't surprise me when, on Thursday night, it was announced that in the morning he was going to head up north for a while, maybe for good. Seemed like the guy had been well-liked and the mood around the clubhouse had been a somber one all fucking week.

I'd spent a couple nights over with Veronica during the week, although we still hadn't had sex yet. She hadn't confided any more details about her past with me, and

Keys had been busy with all the Bash turmoil to spend too much time digging into her history. However, she'd agreed to come to the club barbecue that was going to start soon and spend the night here with me, so I hoped that was a sign she was ready to take the next step.

I couldn't believe I was willingly taking my time with a woman. Never in my life had I needed to work to get laid. Although, I'd never cared as much about any of the other women I'd previously fucked as I did about Veronica. I couldn't wait for her to trust me enough to tell me her history. It tore me up inside that I didn't know how safe she was, because I had no clue who was out there looking for her hard enough she'd had to change her name and run.

"Hey, Blade! Got a minute?"

I turned to see Mac and Scout coming my way. I relaxed when I saw Mac was sporting a grin the size of Texas. Seemed like finally something good had happened for the club.

"Sure, man. What can I do for you?"

"Just got outta church. Some votes were taken." He tapped his chest, over a new patch that hadn't been there before that read Vice President.

I reached out to shake his hand and clap him on the shoulder. "Whoa! That's great, man. Congratulations."

"Thanks, but that wasn't the only thing we voted on."

Scout spoke up. "Club voted to give you the chance to prospect in, if you want it."

That caught me off guard. "What, exactly, does that mean? Because I've seen some of the shit jobs you make prospects do around here and to be honest, I'm likely to throw a punch if I get asked to do some of that shit."

Scout laughed while Mac paled slightly. "Bit like when Mac and his boys prospected in, we'll make use of your skills. Which would be wasted on half the shit we get prospects to do. You're also limited on heavy lifting until that arm heals up. You'll be doing a lot of security work, guarding either businesses or the women. Shit like that. You also need to pick a club business you wanna work in, but you don't need to do that right now."

I gave the man a nod. I could live with that.

"How long till I get to call myself a brother?"

For some reason, that made the man wince. "Ah, normally it takes around a year. We've been slack lately, but with Mac as VP, I got a feeling that won't be an issue going forward."

"Damn straight. Do what you're asked, keep your nose clean and in a year's time, you'll be wearing all your patches."

I rubbed my hand over my beard for a few seconds before I gave them another nod. "Okay, I'm in."

The holler Mac let out was loud enough it echoed around the hallway and had Scout and me chuckling.

"Come with me to my office and we'll get your cut."

I'd picked up soon after arriving that they called their leather vests their cut, or colors. I couldn't help the buzz of excitement that flowed through me as I followed Scout and Mac to the club president's office.

An hour later I stood out the front of the clubhouse, sporting my new leather vest waiting on Veronica. Scout told me I could start my duties tomorrow, but today I could celebrate joining the fold, which sounded like a damn fine idea to me. I couldn't wait to get Veronica up in my room to help me celebrate.

Her little blue hatchback pulled in and by the time she parked it next to the other vehicles, I was over at her door. Impatient to see her, I opened it up and held my hand out to her. She took it and I pulled her up out of her seat and into my arms. Before she could utter a word, I had my lips on hers, kissing her until we were both breathless.

A few whistles had me pulling away.

"Ah, wow. Um, hi?"

Her cheeks were flushed with color and I grinned down at her.

"Hey, my little dove."

She stroked her palms over the leather I was now wearing. "So, this is new…"

"Yep, I'm officially a prospect in the Charon MC now."

"I have no idea what that means, but you look happy, so I take it that's a good thing."

"Well, it means I'm staying here in Bridgewater for good. I'll need to head back to L.A. soon to pack up all my shit and get things finalized, but I'll be coming back here to live."

Before she could respond, a high pitched squeal filled the air and we both turned to see what was going on. Mac had just spun his old lady around in a circle while she held their daughter.

"Guess Cleo liked that."

"Guess so."

As we watched, Mac grabbed Sparrow and gave her a spin too. Even from across the yard I could see the way her face went red, but she was grinning, so all was well.

"Wonder why he's so excited?"

"That's Mac, my buddy. He just got voted in as the vice president of the club. It's a good day. Gonna be one hell of a party. You're still good to stay the night, yeah?"

I couldn't believe I was actually nervous she'd changed her mind.

"Ah, yeah, I brought a bag. Change of clothes and stuff."

Releasing her, I reached past her into the car and grabbed the bag, then shifting her out the way, I shut the door. "Let's get your shit up to my room, then we'll head out the back. Make the most of having me the whole time, little dove. Next time I'll be on duty and have jobs to do before I can relax with you."

Poor woman looked more than a little stunned as I took her hand and brought her into the clubhouse. It wasn't anything out of the ordinary. The main room was just a bunch of tables and chairs with a few couches against the walls. There was also a bar along one wall near where the stairs went up to the upper levels. That's where I took her, up to the second level, where the bedrooms were. She didn't say a word as we made our way down the hallway. No one else was up here at this point, everyone was either out the back or in the main room, relaxing. Suited me just fine. Meant I got to my room quickly and once we passed through the door, I tossed her bag on the chair near the bathroom entrance then had her up against the wall, my body pressed against hers.

"Fuck, I missed you."

I nuzzled my face in against her throat, getting a giggle then a groan out of her. I stroked my hands down her body then back up, catching her shirt on my way, lifting it up and over her head before she knew what I was doing. The blue lacy bra had my dick kicking in my jeans and my mouth salivating for a taste.

"I'm getting the idea blue is your favorite color."

"I have no idea where you'd get that idea from."

I traced a fingertip lightly over the edge of the lace, loving the way goosebumps rose in the wake of my touch. When she shuddered and wrapped her hand around my wrist, I stopped moving and shifted my gaze to her eyes. The moment her eyes locked with mine, her body relaxed.

"We're good, sweetheart. Just me and you here, gettin' to know each other. Say the word and we'll stop, but damn, I'd really like to continue just for a few more minutes. We don't have long before we need to be downstairs in the yard for the start of the celebrations."

She cleared her throat. "I think if I can see your eyes, I'll be fine for a little more."

I grinned then leaned in and pressed a soft kiss to her mouth. "Easily done, my little dove. You keep looking at my eyes, even when I can't resist your body any longer and have to look down, you keep your gaze on mine and we'll see how far we can go."

She nodded and pulled her lower lip between her teeth. I shifted my hands up to push the straps from her shoulders before I slid them behind her back. Kissing her, I flicked open her bra before pulling back. She didn't stop the material from falling from her body and my breath caught. Even looking at her eyes, I could see her gorgeous tits in my peripheral as I filled my palms with the soft mounds. I wanted to look down and focus on them so badly, but I didn't want to lose her to the demons in her mind.

Needing a taste, I lowered down to my knees in front of her, still not losing our connection. Then turning my head, I latched onto a nipple, flicking my tongue over the pebbled tip before sucking it deep in my mouth. With a gasp, her eyes went wide and she lifted her hand to thread her fingers through my hair. When I swirled my tongue around her nipple again, she tightened her grip. As I continued to tease her with my lips and tongue, I flicked the other nipple with my thumb, teasing both at the same time. After a few minutes I switched sides, drawing the sweetest little whimper from her when I gave the nipple I'd just released from my mouth a hard tweak between my thumb and finger.

She was so damn responsive, and her skin tasted as sweet as she smelled. Fuck, I wanted to get my mouth on her pussy something fierce. We didn't have a whole heap of time right now, but fuck it, I needed a taste of her so badly I willingly took the risk that we'd be late to the party. Dropping my hands away, I switched my mouth back to the other nipple, keeping her panting for me as I lowered my hands to the fly on her pants. I got the button undone and the zipper down before she stiffened up.

Releasing her breast, I leaned out a little.

"Let me have a taste, sweetheart? No sex, not yet, but you smell so fucking good, I need to have you down my throat. And since I was the one who got you so worked up, seems only right that I be the one to take care of it for you."

"I've never— no one has ever put their mouth down there."

That had my heart soaring. I'd be the only one who would ever know what it was like to have her taste down the back of my throat.

"That's good, darlin', real fucking good. Means that it's all mine."

Hopefully it also meant I wouldn't hit any triggers. While still keeping my gaze on hers, I slid my hands over her hips, under the material of her jeans and pushed them, along with her panties, down her legs. She still had her shoes on, so I left them around her calves. That would give me enough room for now. Later on, I'd get her naked with her legs around my head as I made a proper meal out of her.

"Just a taste for now, little dove. Later I'll be back down here for a full meal."

I pressed my nose into the crease between her thigh and torso and inhaled against her soft flesh. I pressed a kiss before I pulled away and focused fully on her face for a moment.

"You doing okay?"

She nodded, her eyelids having closed half way with her arousal. Woman was the sexiest thing I'd ever seen and I'd only looked directly at her eyes. I could see the rest of her in my peripheral vision, but couldn't wait for her to be comfortable enough with me that I could look directly at every inch of her body.

Shoving her jeans down as far as I could, I tapped her inner thigh. "Spread them as much as you can. Give me a little room to work."

She wriggled against the wall, bending her knees out to open herself up to me. The scent of her arousal washed over me as she moved. With a growl, I leaned in and took my first swipe up her center.

Fuck. For a moment my eyes slid shut at the Nirvana that filled my senses.

"So good, sweetheart. So fucking good."

I gripped her hips in my hands and locking my gaze with hers once more, I leaned in and ran my tongue between her lower lips again, until I got up to her clit, which I stopped to flick with my tongue before I sucked at it. Her mouth dropped open a moment before her eyes slammed shut and her body went taught as she whimpered and came. Now that her eyes were closed, I hungrily ran my gaze over her shuddering body as I lapped at her core, taking every drop of her cream for myself. I was already addicted to her taste and couldn't wait for later tonight when I could have her on her back in my bed, with my mouth right where it was now.

As my gaze ran over her, I noticed for the first time she had a tattoo on the inside of her right hip bone. As I nuzzled my face against her inner thigh, pressing little kisses to the trembling flesh there, I ran my thumb over the crudely drawn star with an A in the center. On the third stroke over the ink, she stiffened and pulled away from me.

"Whoa, Veronica. It's okay, we're okay."

She already had her panties and jeans tugged up by the time I was on my feet and dragging her back against me.

I wanted to ask who was behind that tattoo but if this was her reaction to me just seeing it, I knew it wouldn't be a discussion we'd be having any time soon.

Tugging her with me, I sat on the edge of the bed and pulled her into my lap, curling her up like I had that first night. She nuzzled into my chest, her palm splayed over my heart. I was wearing a t-shirt today, so I couldn't undo the buttons to give her access. And I sure as fuck wasn't putting her down to strip off, so I grabbed her wrist and lowered it down until she could hook it under the bottom of my shirt. She got what I intended and slipped her hand under the material until it was up over my left pectoral.

Damn this woman was breaking my fucking heart with her vulnerability. How could anyone look at this sweet creature and want to hurt her?

Veronica

After the awkward end to our little session earlier, we'd come down and I'd been surprised to actually have enjoyed my evening. Zara introduced me to the other old ladies and I'd hung out with them for a little while before Blade came and reclaimed me.

A big man with a beard much longer than Blade's short one stood up at one point and made some announcements, including Blade's new status as a prospect. He seemed totally happy with the development, and I had to admit I was glad he would be settling here in Bridgewater. I wasn't sure where, exactly, this thing between us was going, but I really wanted to find out.

My body was still tingling from earlier, even if things did end abruptly when he'd discovered my tattoo. I'd expected him to ask questions, but he hadn't pushed me since that incident outside Marie's Cafe. By the time we'd got back to my place, he'd been in full-on caretaker mode and was still there.

It was now getting late. Many of the old ladies had gone home and there were no more kids running around. That was apparently the cue for a bunch of barely dressed women to join the party. I frowned as they filed out the rear door and spread around the yard, latching on to whatever man would let them.

"Fucking club whores."

I turned to see Silk, whom I'd been introduced to earlier. She was Eagle's old lady and a tattoo artist. After I'd lied and told her I had no ink, she'd spent ten minutes begging for me to let her be the one to pop my tattoo cherry. She'd also had a son with her earlier.

"What? And where's your son?"

"Raven's having a night with the grandies." She paused and nodded to the women. "And I was talking about them. They're the club whores. They're confined to a room inside until ten at night, then they get to roam free. Some of them are all right I guess, but for the most part, they don't care who they fuck. Don't care if they're taken or not. Nor do they care about privacy."

I followed her gaze and stumbled back a step. "Whoa, that escalated quickly."

One of the whores was naked on the picnic table top, a man between her thighs thrusting into her while another man had his dick down her throat.

"Yeah. It does. You staying tonight or heading home? Because if you're heading home, I'd suggest you do that soon. Well, unless live porn is your kink."

Considering I could remember a time when I'd been forced to provide the live porn, I had no interest in watching that shit.

"Definitely not my kink. I, ah, I think I'm just gonna go find Blade then get outta here."

She pressed her hand to my forehead. "You're not looking so great. Hey, look at me, not them. You're doing fine, sugar. They're nothing you need to worry about, 'k?"

"Everything okay, babe?"

Silk turned to Eagle who'd come up beside us but I wasn't tracking what was said. I couldn't believe I was having another episode so soon. So far I'd managed to not let the memories take over, but it was taking everything in me to hold it all down.

The sound of heavy footfalls getting closer to me a few moments later had me twisting my head in that direction. Blade was jogging my way with Eagle at his side. Guess Silk sent her man to go get mine. Blade took my face between his palms and held my gaze.

"We doing okay, little dove?" He didn't look away but spoke to the side. "Silk, what happened, what was the trigger?"

"Club whore getting double teamed over on the table."

He winced. "Fuck. I meant to get you outta here before they came out. Time slipped away from me."

Leaning in, he pressed a kiss to my temple then tucked me in against his front.

He shook Eagle's hand and thanked his friends before he bent and scooped me up against his chest and headed inside. I was back to feeling like I was floating as he took me upstairs to his room. As soon as his door was shut, he gently set me on the edge of the bed before he dropped to his knees in front of me. I watched, detached, as he took my shoes and socks off, giving each of my feet a rub before he set them back down.

"I promised myself I wouldn't push, but, sweetheart, if I knew what happened to you, I could better prevent you from hitting triggers going forward. Just," he sighed heavily, "just know, whenever you're ready, I'm here and all ears, okay?"

He looked up, our gazes locking together and the fog started to lift. My heart ached at the pain in those blue depths, so similar to what I'd seen in them that first day when his burns were still hurting him so badly. I leaned forward, cupping his face in my palms a moment before I pressed my lips to his for a short kiss, keeping my eyes open and locked with his when I pulled away.

"You are such a good man, Jared Walker. Better than I deserve."

He winced. "I'm no prince, sweetheart, but I want to take care of you more than anything else in this world."

"That, right there, makes you my prince, Blade."

I slid my hands down his neck to where I started to push the leather off his shoulders. He wrapped his hands around my wrists before I got very far.

"You sure, Veronica? If you want, I can just hold you while you sleep. If you're not up to it, I can wait."

Tears pricked my eyes at his sweetness. This former mobster, who was now an MC member, was possibly the sweetest man I'd ever met. He'd been so unexpected.

"I'm sure, Blade. Help me burn away some more of those old memories."

He gave me a nod, then rose up to his feet. He carefully removed his vest and hung it over the back of the chair that had my bag sitting on it. Then he pulled his shirt over his head and I got a little breathless taking in all the muscular real estate he'd just revealed. He dropped his shirt then glanced over at me with a smirk and a twinkle in his eyes.

"You gonna join me stripping off, or do you want me to do it for us both?"

Heat flared over my cheeks and I forced my mouth closed from where it had dropped open at some point. I stood awkwardly and went for the bottom of my shirt. As I pulled it over my head, memories tried to encroach on the moment. Tried to remind me of the last time a man made me strip for him. But this was different. I looked up at Blade, desperate to see his bright blue eyes. I had no clue why, but something about them grounded me.

After toeing off his boots and losing his socks, he looked up and with a frown, barreled toward me.

"Veronica, we're fine. It's just you and me here. No pressure. What was the trigger? I need to know so we don't hit it again, sweetheart."

I felt like an absolute fool. Who the fuck freaked out over stripping for their lover?

"Taking my clothes off. He used to make me—"

A lump in my throat cut me off but he didn't push. Just leaned in and pressed a quick kiss to my lips before moving back and running his hands up my sides.

"Well, then, guess it'll just be up to me to unwrap you each time. Trust me, my little dove, I have no problem with that."

As he unclipped my bra, he kissed me again, holding my gaze until I let my lids drop closed as I got lost in the way he was mastering my mouth. I wrapped my arms around his neck as he continued to distract me with his tongue and lips, while his hands set about stripping away the rest of my clothes. By the time he pulled away again, I was naked and panting for him. He stepped back and let his gaze drop to run over my body, and this time he didn't linger on my hip and the ink there but moved straight over it.

"So fucking beautiful, little dove."

He flicked open his fly and after hooking his thumbs in the top, he paused. "You ready?"

His whole body was tense, like he was holding himself in check. I was beyond ready for tonight with him, but I couldn't have him stopping to see if I was okay every couple of minutes. The past was firmly back in its box now, and I refused to allow it to ruin this night.

I stepped up to him and as I spoke, I slid my hands inside his pants and hooked my thumbs under the waistband of his underwear.

"I'm more than ready, but, Blade, you can't keep stopping to check in with me. I know I'm broken, but I don't want to be. Tonight, I need you to help make me feel normal. Before you, I'd never willingly taken a lover. You're my first. I want to be able to look back on tonight and remember how you overwhelmed me, how I couldn't think of a damn thing but you all night long. Not how my past ruined it all."

I shoved his pants and underwear down over his hips. As the material dropped down his legs, a growl rumbled from his chest, making my skin tingle.

"You letting me off my leash? Be careful, love. Once we start, I'm not sure I'll be able to pull back and I can get rough."

I hadn't wanted to, but I had to admit that I was rapidly falling in love with this man, and I knew even if I had a freak-out in the middle of us having sex, he'd find a way to stop, to pull back. Because that was the kind of man he was. Feeling brave, I wrapped my hand around his hard erection, giving it a solid stroke and drawing a full body shudder from him.

"Give me your true self, Blade, not a muted version you think is all I can handle. I think I might just like you getting a little rough."

His head lowered and he looked at me from under his lashes before he growled words out at me. "You're in for it now, my little dove."

He took hold of my wrist, pulling my grip off his erection. Then he had his hands around my waist and I was in the air a moment before landing on the mattress with a gasp. Before I could move an inch, he was on the bed between my thighs.

"Told you earlier that I was gonna make a meal outta you, and I'm a man of my word, darlin'."

With the first swipe of his talented tongue, my eyes nearly rolled back in my head. I'd never felt anything like the pleasure that raced through my body when he touched me like this. I reached out to take handfuls of the bedding as he proceeded to do just as he said he would. Make a meal out of me in the best possible way.

Blade

This woman was going to slay me. She'd been badly abused. I might not have the details yet but it was obvious she had some PTSD going on from whatever she'd been put through. Yet here she was, shattering apart under my tongue and fingers. Fuck me. When she'd taunted me earlier to give her all I had, she'd been offering me everything I'd been wanting to give her since we'd met.

With one last lick up her center, I moved up her body until our faces were level. Her eyes were soft from the orgasm she'd just had, and she was completely relaxed against the bed.

"Fuck, you're gorgeous when you come."

Remembering what she'd told me previously about my eyes, about how if she could see them she'd be fine, I made a mental note to make sure she could see my face no matter what we did tonight. I'd told her I wasn't sure I could pull back if what I did got too much for her, but I knew that was bullshit. The first sign she was freaking out and I'd stop on a dime. No question about it. But I was praying that didn't happen.

I lowered my mouth to hers and plunged my tongue in deep, letting her get a taste of herself. She moaned and her hands slid up my chest and neck until she was cupping my face. She was so damn sweet. I thrust my hips, rubbing my hard cock through her slick folds as I kept kissing her until she was writhing beneath me, wanting this as much as I did.

Tearing my lips from hers, I lunged for the edge of the bed, scrambling to get the drawer open on the nightstand. Pulling a strip of condoms out, I snapped one off and tossed the rest on the top for later. No way was one gonna be enough for tonight. Then I shifted to kneel between her thighs, so I could take her in while I rolled it on. Her gaze was switching between my face and my hands on my cock and I smirked at her as I gave myself a few lazy strokes.

"Gonna make you mine, Veronica. Tell me what I wanna hear. That you're mine."

She ran that tempting little tongue over her lower lip before lifting her gaze to mine from where she'd been watching me work my cock.

"I'm yours, Blade. Only yours."

"Damn straight." I growled the words out so low, I wouldn't have been surprised if she hadn't been able to make out what I'd said.

I gripped her hips and pulled her down the bed, lifting her up in line with my cock. She wrapped her legs around my waist, holding herself up as I released one hand so I could take my dick and press the head against her soft, slick opening. I groaned at the feel of her heat, wishing like fuck that I didn't need to wear the condom. I'd never fucked without one before, but with Veronica, I wanted it. I wanted to know she held my seed within her. Carried it around all day, like a brand, marking her as mine.

I teased her opening for a few moments, sliding the head of my dick back and forth until she was arching her hips, trying to get more of me inside of her. Only then did I re-grip her hips and slam deep within her.

She screamed my name and her back arched off the bed as her tight channel rippled around my length. I leaned forward over her and took a nipple deep in my mouth as I began to move my hips, thrusting in and out of her perfect body. I wasn't going to last long this first time, I'd been too desperate for her. But I wanted her to come again before I did. I moved to flick my thumb over her clit but the moment I made contact, it wasn't arousal that crossed her expression, but fear. Fuck, no way was I letting her demons ruin this. Quickly I abandoned her clit and reached for her left breast, tweaking her nipple hard before I leaned down and nipped at her jawline.

"There's no place for your demons here. They can't fucking have you. You're mine."

With each of my hard thrusts I made sure to grind against her clit, her eyes were wide and her mouth open as she panted, but there were no signs of fear anymore. She was back with me, one-hundred percent. Elation flowed through me. We could do this. I just needed to pay attention and draw her back to me when the demons tried to drag her away. And I had to admit, it made me damn fucking happy that all it took was a little pain mixed in with her pleasure to have her back with me.

"You're gonna come for me, little dove. For. Me. No one else."

She swallowed and the movement of her throat drew my attention. I wrapped my hand around her neck, applying just enough pressure for her to feel me there, and for me to feel her swallowing again. I lowered my face so our noses were nearly touching, our breaths mingling as I continued to shift deep inside her, taking her hard enough that her whole body moved with each penetration.

I locked my gaze on hers, fucking loving how she looked drunk on passion as I sped up my thrusts.

"Come. Right now, come for me."

I tightened my hand on her throat a fraction and her mouth dropped open as her body tensed, but it wasn't fear that had her on edge. Looked like my girl really did like me rough and raw. Her fingers wrapped around my shoulders, and my right shoulder let out a holler in pain as she dug her nails into the edge of the burn but I didn't give a fuck because her core tightened up on me and she came, screaming my name, dragging me with her.

When I could think again, I had my face buried in her neck as my hips continued to slowly pump against her. I'd come harder than I ever had but my cock was still half hard, wanting more of this woman. Realizing she couldn't see my eyes in my current position, I shifted and lifted up to look into her face. I grinned when I saw they were closed, her mouth was tilted up in a small smile.

Reluctantly, I pulled free from her and rolled off the bed. In the bathroom, I quickly disposed of the condom, cleaned myself up then wet a cloth. When I returned, I chuckled softly at the fact she'd not moved an inch. When I pressed the warm cloth against her pussy, she jolted and her eyes flew open.

"What—"

"Just cleaning you up, little dove. Relax, get a little rest. I'll be at you again soon enough." I gave her a smirk as I tossed the towel on the nightstand then pulled her so she was draped over my chest. "Got a feeling I'm never gonna get my fill of your sexy self, so be prepared to not sleep much whenever we spend the night together."

Which, if I had my way, would be every damn night.

I rolled to the side and she snuggled in against me, I was beginning to drift off myself when I heard her sniffle and stiffened.

"Veronica?" With a finger under her chin, I lifted her head so I could see her face. "What's wrong? Did I hurt you?"

She'd appeared to enjoy what we did, but I had gotten rough. I knew a lot of women didn't like their throat to be held like I had held hers.

After licking her lips, she gave me a smile through her tears. "You were wonderful. Perfect. These are happy tears. I honestly didn't know if I could do this—have sex—without freaking out. But with you, I did, and it was so very good. You have no idea how much of a relief that is."

I leaned down and pressed a kiss to her temple as my heart swelled for this woman.

"I got a fair idea, little dove."

Because she wasn't the only one that life had fucked over. Sure, my damage was different than hers, but I hadn't thought I was capable of loving a woman like I did Veronica. I'd loved Josefina, but that had been a different type of love, that of a sibling or parent. This, with Veronica, was so much more powerful and it fucking killed me that I didn't even know her real name. How could I keep her safe when she still held on to so many of her secrets?

I forced that thought away as I looked down at the curvy body wrapped in my arms. Hopefully she would trust me with her secrets soon, so I could prove to her that I was man enough to handle them all and to keep her safe. No matter what the future threw at us.

Elita Sabella

Seeing the call was from Nicolas, my man that I'd sent out into the field, I lifted the receiver to my ear.

"You better be ringing with good news."

"I've located the target. Looks like he's settled here in Bridgewater, Texas. I can also confirm he has a woman. She's a nurse at the local hospital."

My lips stretched into a wide grin. "Excellent."

I glanced briefly at my toy in the corner. Seemed the traitor liked to pull medical people into his web. No matter. A woman of my standing, with the businesses I ran, could always use more people with medical training who wouldn't ask questions. I grinned at my toy, who shuddered against his bonds. Of course, patching up my injured staff wasn't the only thing I had them do. Or, rather, it wasn't the only thing I had done to them.

"What do you want me to do next?"

I tapped one of my long, blood-red manicured nails against my desk. The large, heavy, oak piece of furniture that had been my father's until he'd recently been taken down by a traitor, as I contemplated what to tell Nicolas. "Keep observing for now. Get me all the information you can on his movements, and that of his little nurse. Then, when we're ready to strike, I'll have you grab her and bring her to me. Alive."

"Yes, ma'am."

I hung up the phone and placed it carefully on the desk as my thoughts ran wild. Finally I would get to deliver vengeance against the traitor who took my father from me. As soon as all the other elements I had planned out were ready to go, his house of cards was going to tumble and fall, and I'd be there to watch it all.

A chain rattling from the corner of my office had me turning my attention that way. With another wide grin I stood from my desk, unbuttoning my jacket as I made my way over to my little toy. The high and mighty Dr. Maestro didn't look so full of himself now. Not at all. Naked and shackled, he was here to please me in any way

I wished as penance for helping that good-for-nothing traitor who'd killed my father, the great Antonio Sabella.

"Hmm. I think a celebration is in order. What do you say, boy?"

He whimpered as I ran my nail down the side of his face.

"No words for your mistress? I'm almost saddened if we've broken you so quickly. Stand up."

He stood, and the way he held his head, his jaw clenched hard told me he was far from broken. Good. It was so much more fun to play with them before they became totally lost.

I reached out and cupped his balls and soft cock, playing with them.

"You going to get hard for me, boy? Or are we going to play with other parts of your body today?"

He knew his only options. It was either fuck or be fucked. Either way would be entertaining for me. Watching this man who'd been so very full of his own self-importance getting fucked up the ass by one of my men was glorious to watch.

With a grunt, he squeezed his eyes shut as he started to thicken in my hand. I gave his cock a hard tug and it continued to harden for me. Maybe I'd take him down the hall and invite my men along to join me in this celebration anyway. As I'd said, the news I'd just received was worth celebrating, and until I could get his new little nurse and take her from him, Dr. Maestro would have to do for my entertainment.

Releasing his cock, I gave it a sharp slap before I pulled the key from my pocket and unlatched the chain from the wall.

"Come with me, boy. We have a party to get to."

His whimper was music to my ears as I opened my office door and led him down the hall, calling out to my guards to follow as we passed by them.

The future was looking up.

Chapter 6

Veronica

In the week since I'd first had sex with Blade, we'd spent as much time together as we could. Unfortunately, between my shifts at the hospital and his prospect duties, that wasn't a whole lot. After the second time he'd scared the hell out of me by banging on my door late at night, I'd given him a key. I knew things between us were moving too fast, but it felt so right I was refusing to allow myself to worry about it. I felt so safe with him, I hadn't even considered I couldn't trust him with a key to my home.

So I wasn't in the least surprised when in the early hours of the morning, I woke to find him crawling into my bed. I smiled as I took a deep breath of his scent into my lungs as I ran my fingers over his chest. When I opened my eyes to take him in, I frowned. Even in the low light that my alarm clock provided, I could see his gaze was burning hot and his every muscle was bunched and ready to fight.

"What happened?"

He shook his head. "Later. Right now, I need you. Need to feel you beneath me, know you're safe."

Something had definitely gone down and I wanted to know what it was. More specifically, I wanted to know if he'd discovered who I was and had gone after my uncle.

"You didn't—"

He cut me off with a kiss, thrusting his tongue in against mine with a growl. Keeping at me until I was squirming beneath him as my arousal burned hotter for him.

"We'll talk later. Nothing happened directly related to you. It just fucking reminded me of what could happen. I need you so fucking badly right now. Tell me I can have you. Tell me you're mine."

It was becoming obvious he had an obsession with hearing me tell him I was his. It was becoming obvious I wasn't the only one in this relationship with issues.

I wriggled until I could shift my legs to either side of his hips so his hard erection slid against my core, then I spoke. "I'm all yours, Blade. Only yours."

He shifted his weight to one elbow and lifted the other palm to stroke down my face and over my hair before running it down my arm. Lacing his fingers through mine, he lifted my hand up above my head, pressing it hard into the pillow before shifting his weight to do the same on the other side. Then his lips were back on mine, kissing me deeply as he switched his hold so both of my wrists were trapped in one of his palms. Every time we had sex, Blade took control. Each time he pushed it a little further, and with each new experience he gave me, the memories of the past were driven further and further away.

He lifted my leg so my knee was high against his ribs before he ended our kiss to lean back a little. Taking my ankle in his palm, he raised it to his shoulder so the back of my leg was pressed against the hard plains of his torso. This new position had me wide open to him, which he took instant advantage of as his fingers went straight for my core, toying with the moisture he found waiting for him.

"Hmm, so wet for me."

He kept his gaze on mine as he thrust two fingers inside me, twisting until he found that sensitive spot I'd believed was a myth before him. With a gasp, I arched my back as arousal shot through me like a tidal wave.

"That's it, gorgeous. Sexiest woman I've ever seen, and you're all fucking mine."

He bent his head down to nip at my jaw as he pressed into me again and I flew apart, calling out his name as I came hard.

I was still floating back into myself when he pushed his erection inside me. One hard thrust and he was buried to the hilt. I yelped in shock as his girth stretched my sensitive muscles still recovering from my first orgasm. He let my leg drop down around his waist and he buried his face in against my throat as he started to move. I felt every ridge of him as he shifted in and out of me, slow and deep at first. His free hand slid up my rib cage until he had my breast in his palm. He shifted his mouth to nip and suck on my collarbone as he pinched my nipple. I tugged at my hands, trying to get them free as he sent me hurtling toward another climax with how he was playing my body.

He rubbed his beard over the sensitive spot he'd just sucked before lowering to take a nipple into his mouth. He sucked hard as he pinched the other one and I bucked against him. "Fuck!"

The curse left me on a rush. He was teasing the hell out of me but still fucking me so slowly I couldn't quite go over the edge.

"Blade, please."

With a final lick across my beaded nipple, he lifted his face to look into my eyes. "Please what, gorgeous?"

"Harder, I need you to fuck me harder."

The grin he gave me bordered on sardonic and had my heart rate speeding up before he released my hands and shifted to kneel between my thighs.

"I'll always give you want you need, little dove."

He pulled me off his rigid dick and flipped me over onto my front before I knew what he was up to. With gentle hands on my hips, he pulled me until I was on all fours. He cupped my mound in his palm, slipping three of his thick fingers inside me as he shifted my knees outward and made room for himself. His soft lips trailed kisses up my spine and I trembled from the sensations he was raining down on me.

"This okay, or do you need to see my eyes?"

I shook my head. "I know it's you. Please, don't stop."

"I'm not ever going to stop, Veronica."

Tears stung my eyes at him using my alias. It was a reminder of all the secrets that were still between us, but I didn't have time to dwell on it, because he slammed back into me, going deeper in this position. I dropped my head as I panted through the bite of pain that mixed in with the pleasure. Blade was not a small man, but I wasn't complaining. I loved the burn of him stretching me. How hard he took me, like he couldn't wait to get deep inside.

His fingers bit into my hips as he set up a fast, hard pace, slamming into me. I reached a hand out and pressed my palm against the headboard to stop myself from sliding too far forward. He growled and paused in his thrusts to lean over my body, He was so much bigger than me, he caged me in beneath him. Putting all his weight on one arm, he slide his other palm up my front. When he tweaked a nipple, I clenched down on him with a moan. He had me near mindless with arousal. Then he started to move his hips again, thrusting in and out of my tight channel as his hand rose higher up my body until he had his fingers wrapped around the front of my throat. My pulse hammered against his fingers and he dropped his head against my back as he continued to take me hard and fast, just like I wanted him to.

My body was a live wire, so close to the edge I whimpered with his every thrust. His body trembled against mine, telling me he was just as close. He shortened his thrusts, running the head of his dick over my g-spot with every glide, then he shifted his hand and flicked his thumb over my clit and I was gone.

"Blade!"

Stars filled my vision before it went black, the orgasm was that intense.

Blade

Her body clenched down on me hard as she came and it was all I needed to go over the edge myself. Coming hard and filling her up. *Aw, fuck.* I wasn't wearing a damn condom. There wasn't a damn fucking thing I could do about it now, no way could I pull out when she was so fucking perfect surrounding me. I kept thrusting into her—slow, deep strokes as she melted beneath me into the mattress as she came down from her high. I'd also risked playing with her clit again. Over the week, I'd pushed a few of her limits, seeing if I could erase some of her triggers. I hoped that the fact she didn't freeze up – in a bad way – when I flicked her clit just now meant she'd managed to move past that particular one. I loved making her come and not being able to stimulate her clit with my hands when I was making love to her made that more difficult to accomplish.

Once I was empty, I pulled gently from her, hating how she tensed and winced as I left her body. I knew I was a fucking bastard for even thinking it, but damn, I loved the sight of my cum on the insides of her thighs, marking her as mine in the most primal of ways. Pressing a kiss to her shoulder blade, I slipped from her bed and went to the bathroom to clean up and get a washcloth to clean her. I was careful as I wiped her tender pussy, cleaning away my seed from her despite the fact I'd like nothing more than for her to sleep with me all over her. That there was more of me inside of her would have to be enough to placate my inner beast for now.

Fuck, I hoped she didn't get too mad when I told her that I'd forgotten to wrap up. I'd never done that before. But then, I'd never had a woman I wanted to keep forever, either. If she got pregnant, it was another tie to bind us. Another way I could hold onto her forever.

"Veronica?" I winced as I tried to work out how to voice what I needed to say.

She sat up and took the cloth from my hands, setting it on the bedside table before turning her full attention to me.

"Just say it, Blade. Whatever it is, just let it out and we'll deal with it."

Fuck, but she humbled me. I could see in her face she was expecting me to say something horrible, but she was in warrior mode and wasn't going to let me see she was scared.

"I forgot the condom, sweetheart. I'm so sorry. I've never forgotten to wrap up before and I promise I'm clean."

The smile that lit up her face had me relaxing.

"Honey, stop worrying. I've been on birth control since I was a teen to regulate my cycle, so we're good there, and I'm clean too."

She patted the mattress next to her and I took the invite. Spooning up behind her so I could wrap my arms around her and hold her tightly against me. Assuring myself she was safe and whole.

I'd gone with the rest of the club to go rescue Needles' woman last night. A fucking cult leader had taken her and had her chained up in a fucking basement. Had made her watch as he tortured another male victim. I'd been with the team that had gone upstairs and found his first victim drugged out of her mind, being raped by two of the cult's men. Those images would haunt my sleep for years. I mentally shook my head. They'd just add to the hundreds that already plagued my sleep. But seeing it all had me thinking of Veronica, of what might happen if I didn't get more information out of her about her past. If someone did manage to take her, I wouldn't even know where to start looking. It wasn't good enough. The time had come for her to share her fucking secrets with me.

Her hand slid over my arm, gently brushing over the nearly healed burn scars before lacing her fingers with mine and trying to pull my arm away from her body.

"Too tight, honey."

"Shit. Sorry, love."

I forced myself to loosen my hold, even though it was the very last thing I wanted to do. She rolled over to look up into my face, lifting her hand to run her fingers down the side of my face and through my beard.

"What happened to have you this strung out?"

"We went on a rescue mission last night. A brother's woman had been snatched. We got her back, but the things that we saw there—" I shook my head, squeezing my eyes shut. "We'd been in time to save her, but it got me thinking—if you got taken, I'd have no fucking clue how to find you."

I had to pause to clear my throat. Just the thought of someone taking her from me had my heart tearing apart. I reached over and hit the switch for her lamp before I rested up on my elbow so I could look into her gaze and see her fully.

"I know I said I'd wait till you were ready, but it's too dangerous to wait. I need you to trust me, Veronica. Tell me what I need to know to come rescue you should the worst happen."

Her eyes showed me every emotion I was bringing out. Gone was the contentment our lovemaking had brought her, and in its place was fear and resignation.

"Doesn't matter what you tell me. You're mine. I'm not letting you go. I fucking love you, Veronica. That ain't gonna change, no matter what happened in your past."

Shock filtered through her expression. "You love me?"

I shook my head at myself. Fuck, I had the worst timing. I hadn't meant to blurt that out just now. She deserved a better declaration. I cupped her face in my palm and lowed my lips to hers, taking her mouth gently, with reverence, before lifting away a fraction.

"For the first time in my life, I've fallen. I'm yours, little dove. My heart and soul are yours. And I can't stand the thought I could lose you because I waited to hear your secrets. Please, I'm begging you to tell me what I need to know to keep you safe."

She blinked rapidly, trying to contain tears, but a couple slipped free and I kissed them away, hating that I'd made her cry.

"If I tell you, you have to promise me you won't go hunting him. I know him. What he'd do to you. You're not the only one who's fallen hard here and I can't imagine life without you either, so promise me you will not go running off to take him out. I haven't heard a peep or seen any sign of him in the seven years I've been here. I don't want to bring his attention to me, which chasing him down would do. I'd lose you and end up back under his control. I don't think I could escape him again. He'd make sure to cut off all my means of escape this time."

The spark of happiness that she was falling for me was quickly trampled by all my concerns for her. Who the hell had hurt her? She knew who I'd been, knew what the club I was now a part of was capable of. It killed me she was still so scared of whoever this fucker was. I hated that I had to make this vow and keep it, or I'd lose her.

"I promise to not make the first move against him, but if he or any of his men come anywhere near you, all bets are off. I'd go to the ends of the earth for you, Veronica. Don't ever doubt that."

She took a deep breath then licked her lips.

"Veronica Jones isn't my real name. I was born Victoria Jovan. The only daughter of Donald and Thelma Jovan. I was raised in Greenswood, about an hour northwest of Dallas. My father's older brother, Allen Jovan, is the mayor—"

Rage had my vision turning red as I concluded what the A on her tattoo stood for. "He fucking tattooed you, didn't he? Your asshole uncle fucking inked your skin."

She winced and nodded. "Yeah, had to mark his property. He did that after I escaped the first time."

"The first fucking time?"

She'd gotten away before only to be caught? What the fuck?

She blew out a breath, looking frustrated. "Do you want the whole story, or for me to answer your questions? Either way, this is a one-time deal. I don't want to *ever* talk about this shit ever again."

I took her hand in mine, kissing her palm before putting it over my heart like she'd done a few times when she'd needed comfort. She instantly pressed her hand flat against my pectoral, no doubt so she could feel my heart beat against her. I had no idea why it brought her comfort, but was grateful I could provide her some.

"Sorry, little dove. Give it all to me." *And I'd try like hell to stay quiet.*

"My uncle never married, never had any children. I was the only child in the family, so naturally my uncle came around a lot to spend time with me. He'd always offer to babysit whenever my parents had to both work at the same time, or if they wanted a date night. They had no clue what he was doing." She paused to take another deep breath and dug her fingers into my chest. "He groomed me. As far back as I can remember, I recall him stripping us both down and sitting on the couch with me. Watching movies. Getting me used to his body, to his touch. It didn't turn sexual until I was older. He was slow and gentle with his seduction of me. Pushing me further a little at a time. He'd sit with me and watch soft porn, touching me like they were on the screen, asking me how nice it felt. And coaxing me into the returning the attention to him. As I got older, the porn we'd watch got harsher and his touch was more invasive."

I was going to be sick. Bile rose up my throat and I had to focus to force it down. Veronica's voice had gone monotone, her eyes glassy. She'd disconnected from the story she was telling, for which I was fucking grateful. No fucking wonder she didn't want to tell anyone this shit. That fucking bastard had played a long game, screwing with her body and mind from when she'd been a baby.

"I was thirteen when he first raped me. He told me it wasn't rape. That because he'd taken care of me, got me soft and wet for him before he took me, that I'd wanted it. He'd trained my body to respond to him. It took me six months before I worked up the courage to talk to my parents about it. They were mortified, and assured me it was indeed rape. But my uncle was powerful. We had to be careful. Allen Jovan was already the mayor, and was not an upstanding citizen at all. He was crooked as hell. Had connections and dirt on a lot of people, which he used often to get his way in all things. I highly doubt he got elected honestly. Bribes, extortion, blackmail—you name it, he was involved. It meant we couldn't take it to the police, too many of them were in his pocket. The only thing my parents could think to do was to send me away to boarding school."

My hand ached, I had my fist clenched so hard in the sheets of her bed. I knew I'd regret making that promise to not go hunt that fucker down when I made it, but I had no idea I'd regret it this much. Death was too good for the bastard.

"I got six months of peace there before—" She cleared her throat and her body shuddered. "Before he killed my parents. It was declared an accident. My father lost control of the car and it went off a cliff. But I knew it was my uncle's work. He saw me as his and wanted me back. As my only remaining relative, he got his wish. The state gave him full custody and I was removed from boarding school and brought to his home." She shifted closer to me and I gathered her in my arms, lying on my side with her curled against me. She shifted her hand and pressed her ear to my heart and I stroked her hair while I pressed a kiss to the top of her head. I wanted to say so much, but I didn't want to stop her from talking. Just like she didn't want to ever speak of this again, I never wanted to hear it. Think about it. But I knew I would, I'd be seeing her as a young girl being abused by a monster in my nightmares for the rest of my life. No doubt, just like she did.

Veronica

I could hardly believe I was spilling all my secrets like this, but it was like a flood. Once I started, it all just flowed out of me. I cuddled in closer, pressing my ear to his heart so the steady beat kept me grounded and I could finish this horror story that was my life.

"It got worse once he had full control of me. He did the tattoo himself on my first night back. I was so upset at losing my parents. I knew then it was him who was behind it, but I had nothing to fight him with. I was overwrought with my grief and he had his men hold me down after he stripped me so he could mark my body as his. Then he raped me while they held me down. He let them paw at me and shove their dicks in my mouth while he flicked my clit until I got wet for him. He always made sure I came. He said it wasn't rape that way, if I got mine. But that was bullshit. I believed my parents when they told me he was wrong. Even with all his grooming and conditioning, I knew he was wrong. I didn't want him touching me at all, let alone being inside me. It was horrible. He never let anyone other than himself penetrate me, but the others were allowed to watch him do it and touch me, or take my mouth while he did. It was hell. Pure hell."

Blade's grip had tightened on me. His heart had sped up and I knew he was on edge from listening to what I was saying. It all proved he really did care for me. Not that I'd doubted his words, but with how tight his muscles were and the barely contained fury on my behalf that was radiating off his body, there was no question how he felt.

"I had to meet with the lawyer for my parents' estate. Somehow the lawyer managed to force my uncle into allowing me to see him alone. He wasn't a man who danced to my uncle's tune. He pretended to when necessary, but he went his own way in the end. My parents had told him about me, what my uncle was doing. They set up back-up plans in case sending me away to boarding school didn't work. It was the lawyer who gave me the Veronica Jones identity. I was so young, he thought something close to my real name would help me get used to it. He set it all up. A way for me to escape, someone to drive me into Dallas. He'd wanted to send me to Oklahoma but I didn't want to go that far from home. Texas was all I'd ever known. So he sorted it out that I got a place at a boarding school in Dallas, then he even managed to get me a scholarship to college when I needed it, to study nursing."

"Did your uncle figure out it was him?"

"I don't believe so. I keep my eye on the death notices for Greenswood and haven't ever seen anything. He was having dinner with my uncle the night I slipped away and left. He told me he'd play the part and help him search for me. Hopefully it worked and he didn't suffer like my parents did for helping me."

His hand was stroking my hair and it felt so nice. Being surrounded by his heat and safety was a slice of heaven. Something I wanted desperately to keep forever.

"What brought you to Bridgewater?"

"I was working in Dallas when I saw a couple of my uncle's goons come into the ER. I managed to stay out of their way and line of sight, but knew then that I'd been lucky to not have been found yet. I handed in my notice that day and started looking for something in a less populated area. My uncle would never lower himself to be seen in a small town he didn't control. Bridgewater's hospital had a nursing position available, so here I am."

I pulled away to wipe the tears from my face. I had no idea how long they'd been flowing, had no clue when I'd started crying.

"So, there you go. My whole horrific history is all yours now."

He'd told me whatever I said wouldn't change how he felt, but how could it not? It had certainly changed how I felt about myself.

"None of that was your fault. You know that, right? Your uncle fixating on you, him killing your parents, him abusing you… none of that is your fault. Please tell me you understand that?"

I nodded as I stared into his striking blue eyes that were filled with such guilt.

"I do. It took me a long time to realize it, but I know all his decisions were his alone. I was an innocent child. But why are you looking guilty? You didn't know me back then."

He cupped my face and brought it to his, kissing me slowly with complete gentleness before pulling away and resting his forehead against mine.

"Little dove, you are not the only one with secrets buried in your past. But I think we've had enough of past demons for one night—or morning. I'll tell you all my secrets another day. I need time to process what you told me before we go delving into my own hell. Okay?"

It didn't seem entirely fair and I wanted to know his secrets like he knew mine, but I understood what he was saying. My story was horrific. I'd lived it, so I knew how hard it was to believe such evil existed in the world.

"Come, let's shower and wash all that shit away. Then we'll catch a few hours of sleep."

"Okay."

I let him pull me from the bed and guide me over to my bathroom. I reached in and flipped the tap on while he stroked his large, warm hands over my body. I loved his touch, the way the calluses on his fingers were rough on my skin. Normally it got me wet and ready for him, but this morning it was simply comforting, grounding me back into the here and now after reliving my past.

Chapter 7

Blade

It was later that night after I'd finished my stint guarding the front door that I was in the clubhouse bar tossing back Maker's Mark like it was water, trying to drown out Veronica's words. It had been a busy day at the clubhouse, with Needles proposing to Bess and her saying yes, among other things. Even though it was now edging toward midnight, it was still busy. Most of the old ladies had headed out but the brothers were still partying it up. I'd had to shove three club whores away so far.

I swallowed my next mouthful as someone came up beside me. I swore, if it was another of the whores, I was going to grab a fresh bottle and go drink in my room. I tensed up and turned ready to blast her when I stopped short. It was Keys sitting beside me, sipping a beer and watching me like I was a ticking time bomb.

"What happened?"

I shook my head and took another mouthful, the shit not even burning my throat anymore.

"Veronica told me everything. Made me promise to not go after the son of a bitch before she'd tell me. Regretting that right about now."

"That bad, huh?"

"Worse, Keys. Whatever you're fucking thinking, double it— hell—triple that shit and you might get close."

He nodded slowly as he took another swig of his beer. "Anything we need to know about?"

"Like you said, it's been seven years and he hasn't shown his face. I think she's safe for now, but if we go poking around her past, we might bring him to us."

"Need you to at least give me the basics, Blade. Who we need to watch out for."

I glanced around us, seeing who was in earshot. Everyone was busy with their own shit and the prospect behind the bar had left the bottle of Maker's with me long ago and had taken off to have some fun of his own.

"Real name is Victoria Jovan. From Greenswood. Her parents are dead, thanks to her uncle, who, to say has an unhealthy obsession with his niece is an understatement. Allen Jovan is the mayor up there and as dirty as fuck." I turned to look into the older man's eyes. "Fucker started messing with her when she was a baby, Keys. A fucking baby. Then he killed her parents when they sent her to boarding school to get her away from him. He tattooed his fucking initial onto her when he got her back. Death is too good for this motherfucking piece of shit, but I promised my girl I wouldn't go after him. I wouldn't take the first step. So I gotta sit here with my thumb up my ass, waiting on him to find her so I can take him apart."

"Greenswood is Satan's Cowboy's territory." I'd already met a few of the Cowboys when they'd stopped in at our clubhouse on their way through on a run. They were the biggest club in Texas and their original chapter was in Cutler, not far from Greenswood. "I'll give their president, Viper a call and get him to quietly keep an eye on the bastard. Give us a heads up if he ever makes a move in this direction. It might take time, but we'll get 'em and keep your girl protected."

He finished his beer and stood to go get himself a glass, pouring himself some Maker's and refilling mine.

"Hate to have to tell you this after the day you've had, but I only just saw it. Been so fucking tied up with dealing with this shit over in Rocky Gully I hadn't checked the news sites for a few days. Finally got a chance today."

I paused before taking another mouthful and put the glass down before looking back to his face as a cold shiver ran down my spine.

"What did you find?"

"Missing doctor and nurse in L.A. Same ones that treated your burns."

I glared at the man. "How the fuck do you know who treated me?"

He gave me a big shit-eating grin. "Boy, I know everything, didn't you know?" he paused for a moment but when I didn't respond other than to keep glaring at him, he rolled his eyes and started explaining. "When Mac reported in after y'all got back, he included the hospital name along with Nurse Lilly and Dr. Maestro's names. Mighty big coincidence that they're the two kidnapped, dontcha think?"

I closed my eyes and my heart sank. "It's no coincidence. Whoever has taken over from Antonio Sabella is coming after me, taking out anyone who helped me. We need to keep an eye out around town for suits. *Fuck.*"

"Already got prospects guarding the hospital. Didn't put you on that roster because I didn't want to scare the hell out of Veronica. She won't ask the others, but if she saw you there, she'd ask questions and if she's as flighty as you say she is, she'll most likely bolt."

"I need to make some calls and probably go back, see what I can find out. Might as well pack up my shit while I'm there."

Keys gripped my shoulder. "You make those calls, but you won't be alone in going to California. You're a Charon now, Blade. You'll never be alone again. Got me?"

I heaved a sigh and blew out a breath. "I got you. Fuck..." I scrubbed my face as I tried to get my brain working through all the alcohol I'd thrown at it tonight.

"You wanna crash here, or get to Veronica? Because, take it from a man who's been married a long damn time, don't leave her alone after what she's revealed. She'll take that shit as you rejecting her."

Seeing there was only quarter of an inch left in the bottle of Maker's, I poured it all into my glass and took a large mouthful. Would she think that if I didn't see her? I pulled my phone out and tried to unlock the fucking screen.

"Dammit."

Keys lifted it from me with a laugh. "What you wanna tell her? I can take you over there, or I can let her know you're gonna crash here."

I scrubbed a palm over my face. I knew I should probably just head upstairs, but I couldn't. I couldn't leave her alone tonight after what she'd told me this morning.

"Take me to her, Keys. I need to be with her."

He tapped away at my phone before handing it back.

"Done. C'mon, let's get you to your woman so I can get home to mine. I'll come pick you up in the morning and we can get started on planning this shit out. Tonight, you need to rest up and let your liver recover."

Smartass. My liver was just fucking fine. And to prove it, I tossed back the remainder of my drink, because there was no sense in wasting Maker's, then I followed Keys outside to one of the club's cars. The drive over to Veronica's was silent until it occurred to me I'd never told Keys where she lived.

"How'd you know where her house is?"

"Because I looked it up so I could set up cameras to keep an eye on her after you first spoke to me about her."

His tone was all *you even need to ask.* The man really was paranoid about keeping everyone safe. Made me wonder what the fuck was in his history that made him the way he was, but I had enough shit on my plate between my demons and Veronica's, I didn't need to go delving into Keys' for more.

We pulled up and the light was already on. The door opened, revealing Veronica wrapped up in a bathrobe and looking worried. Felt like I was coming home to my wife and was about to be handed my ass for staying out too late and drinking too much.

"Thanks, man. I've got it from here."

When it took me two goes to catch the door handle, Keys laughed. "You sure about that? I can help you up to the house. Damn, but that last drink really hit home, huh?"

With another laugh, he got out of the car and came around to my side. Bastard. No way was I gonna need help to get out of a damn car. I pulled on the door release and stumbled out, but managed to stay upright. Clearing my throat, I glared at him while he continued to laugh at me as I made my way, weaving around a bit, to where Veronica stood waiting for me. I vaguely heard Keys pull away as I slipped past Veronica into her small house. We didn't need to provide her neighbors with any more entertainment tonight.

I left her to lock up and headed straight for her bedroom. I stopped in the doorway and looked at the bed. Perfectly made up on one side, while the other was turned down, as though she'd gotten up in a rush when she'd gotten the text from Keys. Hearing her soft footfalls in the hallway, I turned and watched her come slowly toward me.

"Fuck, darlin', I'm sorry for waking you up. I shoulda just crashed at the clubhouse but I wanted to see you. Sleep beside you."

Fuck, I needed to stop talking. Damn Maker's. I clenched my jaw as she came to stand in front of me.

"Were you trying to drown out what I told you?"

I drank her in. Her soft golden irises, so similar to the color of the whiskey I'd been drinking, her dark curls that were coming to life. She must straighten it every morning to keep it that way, but now that I'd spent a few nights with her I knew it was naturally curly. Fuck, but I'd love to see it in its full glory. "Among other things." I reached up and wrapped a curl around my finger. "Why do you get rid of them?"

She shrugged. "To look different from how I was."

Part of her mask. "Would you leave it natural for me tomorrow? Let me see the real you."

Her expression softened as she ran her gaze over my face.

"It's been a long time since I've let my hair do its own thing. I'm not working tomorrow, so I guess I can. But, Blade, you've seen more of the real me than anyone else on this earth. My hair isn't that important."

I stared at the curl that had fought against her attempts to tame it. It was a tight curl, her hair was thick. My gaze took in all her hair, imagining what it would look like if all of it were curly.

She shook her head. "You're drunk and fixating. C'mon, let's get into bed. I need to sleep, not worry about my damn hair."

Shrugging out of her robe, she stepped around to her side of the bed. She had a cute, lacy camisole and short set on. I couldn't wait to get it off her, but not tonight. I wouldn't give her a sloppy, drunken fuck. She deserved so much better than that. I tried to unbutton my shirt but growled when I couldn't get the fucking buttons through the holes. I was about to simply rip the thing off when her hands gently pushed mine out of the way and did the job for me.

In comfortable silence, I allowed her to care for me, to strip away my clothes until I was in nothing but my boxer briefs. Then she took my hand and led me to the bed. She pulled back the covers on my side and before she could stand back up, I gripped her hips and guided her onto the mattress. She shuffled over and I followed her. She reached over and turned out the light before returning to me. I gathered her close against me and my whole being settled when she pressed her palm over my heart and relaxed against me.

I was right where I was meant to be. I pressed a kiss to temple before I closed my eyes and let myself follow her into sleep.

Veronica

I took in the man lying beside me. Still sound asleep, his hand rested on my stomach under my camisole. I loved the feel of his hands on me. He was so much bigger than I was, rougher. I ran my gaze up his arm, over the healing burns. He'd always bear the scars from whatever had happened that led to him being burned. I really wanted to ask him about it. He knew all my dirty secrets now, but he'd given me very little. The only deeply personal thing he'd told me was that he'd been sold to the mob as a teen. While that in itself was huge, it was the smaller details I wanted. What had he survived? I wanted to know the things that had forged Blade into the man that lay next to me.

My mind ran over last night. I'd been lying in bed, unable to sleep because I'd been worried that I'd scared Blade off forever by telling him what I'd lived through when I'd received the text. I'd been so fucking scared to open that message, afraid it was him telling me he was done with me. But it hadn't been him at all. It had come from his phone, but it had been Keys, Donna's husband, texting to say he was bringing my drunk man to me.

In moments, I'd been wrapped in a robe and waiting by the front door. Chewing my nails, I'd pondered why such a controlled man like Blade had gotten drunk. We'd known each other for less than a month, but I'd never seen him drink to excess before, and doubted it was in his nature to get drunk regularly. He liked being in control way too much to voluntarily lose it. It was just one more thing I didn't know about him. It seemed there were a whole lot of things I didn't know.

Once he'd been dropped off and had made it inside, he'd asked me about my hair of all things. I'd been straightening my hair every morning since I'd left my uncle's home. It was an easy way to make myself look different. My curls were tight and my hair was thick. It would just about be an afro if I cut it short. But straight, it was long and hung down close to my face, and I was a new person that easily.

I picked up a curl that had bounced back to life overnight and held it in front of my eyes. It had been seven years with no sign of him. Maybe I could let it go, leave my hair curly. Heaven knew it would give me more time in the mornings if I didn't have to straighten the damn stuff every day.

A deep groan had me looking back to Blade. His face scrunched up and he took the hand from my stomach to rub his eyes as he groaned again and I smiled. It was human nature to tease someone with a hangover.

"Morning, sunshine."

That got me a grunt before he lifted his hand and glared at me. "Not funny, little dove."

I shrugged, and trying not to grin, leaned over to kiss his cheek. "I'll go get you some Advil."

He gave another grunt as I rolled over and slipped from the bed then went to the kitchen to get the Advil and a glass of water for him. When I got back, he was flat on his back, his arm over his eyes, and the sheets down around his waist. A wave of arousal tingled through me, landing between my thighs as I took in his muscular chest and abs. Clearly the man spent a considerable amount of time in the gym to keep his body in such good shape.

"Like what you see?"

Heat raced over my cheeks. "It's not bad." I walked up to his side of the bed and placed the pills and water on the nightstand. "There you go."

I turned and went to head to the bathroom, but before I made it more than a step or two, his arm wrapped around my middle and he pulled me back. He'd shifted to sit on the edge of the mattress then moved me so I was standing between his thighs, facing him. His hands were wrapped around my hips and he pressed his face between my breasts, nuzzling a little against the lace that covered me, lighting me up when I didn't think he was up for any fun and games this morning. I stroked my hands gently through his thick dark hair as he pulled back and dry swallowed a couple tablets before returning to press against me. His hands slid easily over the satin covering my hips, running his fingertips under the edge, but not trying to push them down.

"I wish we had more time…"

I froze, my hands stilling. Was he breaking up with me? I tried to take a step away, but his grip tightened on my hips and he looked up, frowning.

"What's wrong?"

"I can't do this. I confessed everything to you yesterday and now you want to break up with me?"

I knew I had tears streaming down my cheeks, but I didn't care. My heart was shattering.

"Whoa." He stood in a rush, cupping my face and looking me directly in the eyes, holding me captive with that striking blue gaze of his. "Veronica, I'm not breaking up with you. You have me hooked so hard, I don't think I could ever give you up. I was meaning that Keys will be here soon to pick me up so we don't have enough time for me to lay you out and make a meal out of you, then get inside you."

"Oh."

As relief swept through my heart and my nipples peaked at his final words, heat bloomed in my cheeks at the fact I jumped to the wrong conclusion so quickly. He swiped the tears from my cheeks, then kissed me, pressing those delicious, soft lips of his against mine as he soothed me with his kiss. I slipped my palms up the smooth skin of his torso until my right one rested over his heart and I could feel the steady beat of his heart. He broke the kiss and wrapped his arms around me, pulling me in against his hard body.

"It looks like some shit has come up back in L.A. that I'm going to have to go check out. Not sure when I'll head off, but it'll probably be in the next day or so. I'm going to pack up my place while I'm there so I can get everything moved here. Hopefully it won't take more than a couple of days, and I'll be back in town. While I'm gone, the club will have someone watching you, making sure you stay safe. So if you see anyone with a Charon

MC cut following you around, it's nothing you need to worry about, okay?"

I stiffened in his embrace for a moment before I pushed against him until he loosened his grip enough I could look up at his face.

"Why would I be in danger? Is this something to do with your past, or mine?"

With a wince, he squeezed his eyes shut, then leaned down to press his lips against my temple before shifting to sit on the bed, taking me with him so I straddled his lap, facing him. His palms stroked up and down my arms and back.

"This one is on me, little dove. I don't have time to tell you everything right now. The abbreviated version is that in order to leave the mob I had to take out someone powerful. It would appear someone else has taken his place and is coming after me." He hesitated, looking like he didn't want to tell me whatever came next.

"Tell me. I need all the information so I can know if I'm in trouble or not. You know all my past secrets, Blade. Trust works both ways."

He nodded and winced again. Then he blew out a breath and spoke words that had my blood running cold.

"I was part of a team that took out the head of the L.A. mob. Antonio Sabella had been my personal boogie man since I was sixteen. It was freeing to take him out. Took out his fucking brothel. We burned it to the ground so no one else could get the information to start that shit up again."

"Your burns."

He nodded. "I slipped, spilling gas down my arm and side. The guys took me to a hospital for treatment when it happened. Keys told me last night that the news has reported a doctor and nurse have gone missing. The same doctor and nurse who treated me."

My world spun. I wasn't sure how the hell to respond to what he'd just said.

"You think whoever this is will come for me because I treated you?"

He shook his head. "They'll come after you for more than that reason. If they know about you, they'll know how much time we've spent together. They'll know you're mine. So, I'm going to head to L.A. to deal with this shit, and the club is going to make sure you're taken care of while I'm gone."

My heart was racing as my thoughts swirled. I should run. Move on to a new town. Maybe get another identity. Start over. Make sure to not ever get involved with a man again.

His eyes went hard a moment before he cupped my face again. "You will not run away, Veronica. If you don't feel protected enough to stay here, you can stay in my room at the clubhouse while I'm away. One of the brothers or prospects will give you a ride to and from work and we'll make sure you're safe."

I shook my head as much as I could in his grip. "No, I don't want to be confined to the clubhouse. I'm comfortable here. I have lots of security and I'm always careful. Always check the cameras before I go outside." I smiled at his shocked expression. "The silver lining to having lived on the run from my uncle for so long is that I'm kinda paranoid."

He chuffed out a laugh. "You and Keys will get along so well. He has half the town wired with cameras. Man knows just about everything that goes on in Bridgewater. The guys down at the clubhouse were telling me he was the one who found Scout's little girl when she ran off because he'd put trackers in her shoes and a few of her favorite toys."

I grinned at that one as I gave him a nod. "That's totally something I'd do."

He leaned in to kiss me again when a loud knock on the door sounded, breaking the moment. He gave me a quick kiss before lifting me to my feet and heading out to answer my door while I grabbed my robe so I could go have a chat with Keys. I wanted to know how he'd placed cameras everywhere without anyone noticing them. Hopefully he'd be able to help me change out the ones I had around my house so if someone did decide to sneak up on me, the cameras would be well hidden and unavoidable. One of my biggest concerns was that someone well-trained would easily detect my amateurish attempt at home security.

Blade

On the short drive over to the clubhouse, Keys stayed quiet as though he knew I was lost in thought. Thoughts about Veronica, about her past, along with my own, crowded my thoughts. My main focus was on who the fuck could have taken over for Antonio Sabella. He had a wife and two kids, but the son didn't take after his father at all. He was more like his mother—gentle and not at all suited to mob life. I highly doubted he would have stepped up. I hadn't seen his daughter in years. She'd gone to NYC for college and as far as I knew, had stayed there afterward, so I doubted it was her. It definitely wasn't his widow. She'd hated what her husband did for a living.

When Keys pulled up outside the clubhouse, I hopped out and walked with him over to the door.

"Your woman is something else. She actually asked me to bug her phone and put a tracker on her shoes. Seriously, why the fuck did she ask me to tag her shoes?"

I chuckled with a shrug. "I mentioned how I'd heard the story about you finding Ariel after she ran off because you had tracked her shoes."

"Ah. Right. Makes sense now. And yeah, I totally tagged her shoes. I've done the same to all the kids. Already got Ashlynn covered."

Ashlynn's father, Needles, had just patched in as a prospect, but like me, he was on the accelerated prospect program. He'd been a fully patched in brother with the Satan's Knights MC up in New York before he got called home to Texas to deal with the con man that was trying to take his mother for all she was worth. That was who'd kidnapped his woman who we'd all gone in to rescue Friday night.

Never a dull fucking moment in an MC it seemed. As proven by the fact we were about to plan a trip over to California to help me deal with my past shit, while that fucker, Godfrey, who we'd caught Friday night, was still in the club's basement, waiting for his judgment to be served.

And I thought my life in the mob had been intense. At least the Charons fought for the innocents. They might do some seriously questionable shit, but they did it for the right reasons. Like saving Needles' woman, Bess, and the others that fucker Godfrey had been holding.

I shook my head. What that bastard had done to those young women and man would cause them a long, fucking time to recovery. If they could.

Again, the Charon MC had stepped in to help. Scout had declared all three of Godfrey's victims were welcome to live in Bridgewater and could be secure in the knowledge they were safe and protected here.

I had no clue if any of them would take up Scout on his offer. All three were still in the hospital for physical and/or mental treatment. I shook those thoughts free. I had more pressing concerns right now.

I followed Keys inside and we headed to the kitchen and got ourselves a coffee each before we came back out to the main room. It was thankfully late enough all the stragglers from last night's festivities had woken up and moved on. Early morning on the weekends the main room looked like a fucking frat house, with club whores and brothers all over. I was glad they'd cleared out already. The last thing I wanted to see this morning was naked club whores and men.

Scout stood as we came in. "Good, you're here. Right, Blade, Bank, Nitro, Machete and Keys, get your asses into church now."

I raised an eyebrow as I followed Scout and the others to the meeting room. A man didn't normally get to enter that space until he was a fully patched in brother. Copying the others, I put my phone and other shit into a locker. Then I couldn't help but feel the moment in my bones as I crossed the threshold.

The table up the front had seats for the officers, while the rest of the room was rows of seats facing the table. There was an aura to the place that made it so much more than the simple set-up it was.

"Take a seat, men, let's get this party started."

We all followed Scout's order quickly. Along with Scout, Nitro and Keys took seats from behind the table and plonked them in front of it to sit in. The rest of us sat in the front row and waited for the club president to start.

He grinned at me. "Welcome to your first time in church, Blade. Prospects don't normally step foot in here until after they're patched in, but this room is the safest place to talk freely. Keys, explain what you've dug up."

Keys cleared his throat and glanced at me before he started speaking.

"As you all know, we went over to L.A. a month ago and with Blade's help, we took out Antonio Sabella, the head of the L.A. mob. Blade suffered some burns that required him to be hospitalized. We didn't go in with our colors flying, but Blade set shit up so we knew the chances of some blow-back were high. I've been watching the media coming out of California, and yesterday I found something. The doctor and nurse who treated Blade have gone missing."

Nitro interrupted, "How long?"

"Five days. There's been no contact made with their families, no sign of them either online or out in the world. Their bank accounts are untouched."

Scout cut in. "Someone is holding them, and not for ransom from their families. We're thinking this is about Blade. Whoever stepped up to take over from Antonio is out for blood. Blade, anyone come to mind for who'd take over?"

I scrubbed a palm over the back of my neck while I racked my brain. "I can't think of anyone that we didn't take out last month."

"What about his kids?"

I shrugged. "Son doesn't have it in him. He's not built for mob life. The last I knew about the daughter was she was living in New York, but who knows? Maybe, Antonio just made sure I never saw her around."

I'd had no fucking clue he'd been holding Josefina for all those years, so maybe I was wrong about the daughter. I looked at Keys. "You find anything on his wife or either of his kids?"

He gave me a nod. "Rosa and Marco, the wife and son, cleared out of L.A. after Sabilla died. Guess his old lady was looking for an out and took the one we gave her. Marco is young, still in college. He's studying architecture. From everything I've found, they both look like they're moving on and not looking back."

The hair on the back of my neck tingled. "What about Elita?"

"She's in L.A. and it looks like she's got her own little business going. My gut tells me this kidnapping shit is her. Looks like Antonio helped her set shit up a few years back and she's been building her own little empire. Guess she was the one who took after her father, rather than the son, but the mob would never have accepted her as their head, so daddy dearest gave her a side hustle."

"Fuck. I knew so little…"

Bank slapped my shoulder. "Don't be so hard on yourself. You knew enough for us to take him out and shut down that fucked-up warehouse of his. You knew enough to save Sparrow. Sabella wasn't a fool, he knew you were only with him because he had you over a barrel. Of course he was going to keep shit from you."

Scout nodded. "Exactly. What do you know about Elita? Ever been to her compound?"

My shoulders slumped in defeat. "I didn't even fucking know she had a damn compound. I saw her a few times, but tried to ignore her. She's an entitled, rich fucking brat."

"With power. Just fucking great. Woman with a god complex coming after you, and us, looking to avenge her bastard of a father." Scout paused to shake his head. "Keys and I are staying here, but the rest of you are heading to L.A. in an hour. Keys will keep digging into this shit, and keep you posted with any new information he finds. Take a van. You might as well pack up your shit and bring it back with you while you're there, Blade."

He stood, grabbed the gavel and pounded it once on the table. "Go say your goodbyes before your trip, men. No fucking clue how long it'll take you, but we have a responsibility to find that nurse and doctor. Their current situation is on us. Let's do what we do best and go deliver some fucking justice, Charon style."

Chapter 8

Blade

It had taken a day and a half to get to my hidden place in Moreno Valley and when we'd rolled up to the trailer, I'd been looking forward to getting inside and out of the blistering sun. Maybe find a little privacy to check in with Veronica. But the second I went to unlock the door only to discover the lock had been busted, I knew shit wasn't going to be pretty.

"On alert, men. Someone's been here, and no one outside of the Charons should know about this place."

Nitro pulled his gun and flicked off the safety. "Machete—with me, around the back. Bank, stick close to Blade."

I pulled my own side arm as did Bank, then with my back against the wall beside the door, I reached over and shoved it open with a quick movement that only left my arm out in the open for a few seconds. When no gunfire greeted me, I risked looking around the door jam and gagged as I cursed.

I stepped into my trailer and glanced around the main living room and kitchen, waiting for Nitro and Machete to come in from the back before I went near the mess on my fucking coffee table. Once all four of us stood in the hallway, I nodded to the living area.

"Found the nurse."

"Ah, fuck. Dammit."

Nitro was the only one who spoke out loud, but I was certain we were all saying worse in our minds. The poor woman had died hard for the crime of caring for my wounds that day last month. Her dead, glassy eyes were focused on the door, as though she'd died on my table waiting for rescue. Guilt tore through me and I turned and strode down the hallway and out the back door. Putting my gun away, I pulled out my phone and started making a few calls to the men who I'd worked with that weren't evil, fucking monsters.

It took five calls before I got someone to answer.

"Man, you shouldn't be calling. Go find a rock to hide under and don't ever come out."

It wasn't much of a greeting, but it was what I'd expected from him.

"Can't do that. Just found the dead nurse on my fucking table. You know where the doc is that she took?"

"Elita is rather fond of her new toy. There's nothing you can do for him, Blade. His fate is already sealed. She's got men out looking for you. Sent Nicolas to Texas to follow your trail."

Panic lit my blood. "When? When did she send him to Texas?"

"Day after her father's body was found in that car."

"Fuck. I gotta go. Thanks."

"Go bury yourself somewhere, man. It's the only way you'll survive her warpath."

I hung up. I couldn't do that. Couldn't leave that doctor in her hands, and there was no way I would leave Veronica vulnerable to Elita, either. She'd been through enough already, the last thing she needed was my past to come hunt her down.

I pulled up Keys' number in the secure app he'd told me to use and hit dial. "Found the nurse."

"Where and in what condition?"

His voice was all business, which I appreciated. "Dead on my coffee table here at my apparently not-so-secret place. Front door was busted open. We've cleared the property and no one else is here."

"Fuck. I'm not surprised, but dammit. That woman was a fucking innocent."

I couldn't agree more with him and Elita would pay dearly for this stunt, but that wasn't my priority right now.

"After finding her, I rang a man I know is solid. He told me Elita sent someone to tail me. He's in Texas. I need to know Veronica is all right."

"Have you tried to call her?"

I shook my head, even though he couldn't see me. "No, I'm too worked up. She'll know something's wrong and panic, probably run off. She's still skittish. I can't spook her, but I need to fucking know she's okay."

"All right. Let me bring up the feed from the camera outside her place."

I listened as he tapped at his laptop, pacing while I waited for him to say something. I stopped in my tracks when he cursed.

"Something's up on her street. Cops and reporters all over the fucking place."

"Can you tell who's house they're in front of?"

"Not from the camera's angle, and I don't have sound. I'll head over there to check it out and get back to you."

He hung up and I continued to pace the backyard, fear and anger mixing within me until I felt like I was going to explode if I didn't find some way of venting it. I was aware that the other men had come to stand at the rear of the trailer, but they stayed silent as I continued to move, cursing under my breath as I waited for Keys to call me back.

When my phone finally rang, I couldn't answer it fast enough.

"Talk to me?"

"Brother, she's gone."

I froze. Couldn't move, couldn't fucking breathe. I heard Keys speaking but couldn't process the words. Veronica was gone. Elita had grabbed her. Planned to torture her in order to hurt me. My gaze cut to Nitro as he approached me with his palms up in surrender, like he knew I was on the edge.

"Give me the phone, Blade. Let me help."

I still couldn't move. The shallow breaths I struggled to take were the only movement my body made. Nitro reached up and slid the phone from my hand, lifting it to his own ear to talk with Keys. Within seconds, his eyes widened and fury clouded his features. The lockdown on my body shattered and closing my eyes, I lifted my head and roared out the pain and fury swirling within me. The sound of the birds flying from the trees around the trailer barely registered as my soul ripped wide open.

My woman, my fucking heart, had been taken. Was no doubt being hurt right this moment and I knew nothing about where she was or how to get to her. Visions of Josefina dying in my arms and the nurse's body that still lay on my fucking table flashed behind my eyes as I fell to my knees.

Veronica

Thanks to my chat with Keys, I now had new cameras to install around my place. Smaller ones that would be hard to spot. With what Blade had told me, I wanted them in place and working as soon as I could. Especially now that I was watching for threats from two sources. Ideas of running away and starting over again plagued my thoughts since Blade had left me yesterday morning. But I'd promised him I wouldn't, so here I was, turning my little house into even more of a fortress than it already was. After finishing with the second camera, I moved down the ladder and began to mentally plan where the next one would go. I'd been so focused on my task, I hadn't noticed I wasn't alone. Stupid mistake, and one I knew better than to make.

A thick arm wrapped around my waist and hauled me off the last rung of the ladder. I opened my lips to call out but before I could, a palm was over my mouth.

"Scream and I'll snap your pretty little neck."

I tried to calm my heart rate down, to assess the situation. Find some way to escape. I couldn't see the man holding me, but his accent sure as fuck wasn't Texan so I assumed this had to do with Blade's past, not mine. He removed his hand but kept his arm tight around my waist, holding me firmly against his front.

"Who are—"

A sting at my neck cut off my words and panic had me forgetting his threat about breaking my neck. I thrashed against his hold, trying to break free. I thrust my elbow back into his torso, kicked my foot back into his leg. With a curse, he released me and I bolted away from him. At least that was my plan, but within a few steps I stumbled and fell to the grass.

"Always the hard way."

Being slung over the man's shoulder was my last thought before my world went black.

My awareness returned to a whopper of a headache, a foul taste in my mouth and an oxygen mask over my face. Remembering how I'd been snatched, I was careful to not move or make a sound despite the pain I was in. Lying flat on my back on a hard surface, I slowly flexed my arms and legs to test if I had any movement. I didn't. It felt like I had wide straps over my wrists and ankles holding me down. I was grateful that I could feel something covering me, but the fact I wasn't wearing pants or underwear had my heart rate ticking up a few notches. I wasn't sore between my legs so I prayed that was a sign I hadn't been raped while I was unconscious.

Forcing myself to ignore my nudity, along with the pain that continued to bang around my skull, I opened my eyes to slits to see what was going on around me. And jerked against the table when I saw a scruffy, bearded man leaning over me, eyes trained on mine.

"Shut your eyes and keep them shut. If you know what's good for you, you'll play along and make like you're still unconscious."

I was about to open my mouth to try to talk through the mask to ask him to explain what he meant, who he was and where we were, when I caught the small sound of a door lock snicking. Seeing the fear in the man's gaze, I decided to follow his orders and slammed my lids closed and did everything in my power to appear asleep.

A minute later, a woman's voice filled the room, her accent all spoiled, rich, valley girl. "My new toy is still sleeping? Seriously? Wake her up, boy."

"I can't just will her awake. You're lucky she's breathing after the amount of drugs your thug pumped into her."

The clicking of heels on concrete came closer and moments after a wave of cool air hit my arm, warm fingers slipped around my wrist. *Please let my pulse be steady.*

"There's a pulse." She released my wrist but didn't bother covering my arm back up, making me think it was the doctor I could thank for having anything over me. When her fingers grasped my jaw, it took everything I had to not react to her painful grip. She turned my face back and forth roughly before releasing me. "The moment she wakes, I want to know. Call out to the guard at the door the second she opens her eyes."

The clicking heels retreated and the door snicked as it closed and, at a guess, locked. I still didn't dare open my eyes again. I had no clue if there were new people in the room who had come in with the woman and not left.

"It's safe to open your eyes now. She won't be back for another hour."

I blinked my eyes a few times to clear them and took in the man as he flipped the sheet back over my exposed arm. He had thick cuffs attached to his wrists, but I couldn't see anything connected to them. Other than that, the man was naked and showed clear signs of abuse. Bruising and welts covered him. What really made my breath catch were his eyes. They looked hollow, like whatever inner fire had once animated them had been extinguished by all he'd suffered. He removed the mask from my face and the moment I was free from it, I started speaking.

"Who was that? Who are you? Where are we? And why'd you just lie to her for me?"

With slumped shoulders he fiddled with the IV that was inside my elbow.

"That vile woman is Elita Sabella, the current head of the L.A. mob and we're at her compound. No idea where it is exactly, but I assume not too far from Los Angeles. I am Dr. Maestro, and I lied to, hopefully, save us both some pain. So long as I'm working, she leaves me be. The moment she realizes you are awake, both of our lives will become hell. Do you know if someone will come looking for you? Because realistically, I can probably only fake your condition for another day at the most. Thankfully, Elita has no medical training, hence her not picking up your no doubt accelerated pulse, but no one will believe you would stay under for so long without further drugs administered, even after the overdose."

My mind spun. The mob had me. This was worse than my uncle. That woman hated Blade enough that she'd chased him across three state lines. And I'd helped him, fallen in love with him. Tears pricked my eyes as my still pain-filled and foggy mind began to draw conclusions.

"You treated Jared Walker's burns, didn't you? Where's the nurse? Is she here too?"

His color paled so much I feared he was going to pass out.

"Lilly is gone. They took her away and I haven't seen her since. I am quite certain she is dead, and that it was not a fast or easy death. And yes, we were taken because we treated Mr. Walker's burns." He paused and frowned down at me. "Who are you to him?"

"I'm a nurse in Bridgewater, Texas. Where Blade — Mr. Walker — ran to after leaving L.A. I'm worse than you, though. I didn't just treat him, but went on to have a relationship with him." I paused to lick my lips. "He will come for me. For us. He's riding with an MC – motorcycle club – now, and they were on their way to L.A. to look for you and Lilly when I was taken." My mind cleared some more and I glanced around the room looking for my discarded clothing. I grinned when I spotted them, along with my sneakers. "They'll know exactly where we are as soon as they realize I'm gone."

"How can you be so sure?"

I nodded over to the pile of my stuff. "I asked them to put trackers in my shoes. How long have I been here?"

"You asked them to do what?" He shook his head. "Never mind. It's hard to tell how much time has passed exactly. It's not like they bring regular meals or allow me a watch." This little room of ours didn't have a window either, just a vent high up on the back wall. "I would guess two days. I wasn't lying to Elita about you being lucky to be alive. They overdosed you when they took you. At a guess, they have doses set for large men, not tiny women."

That explained the bad taste in my mouth. "You gave me activated charcoal?"

He nodded. "Yes, plus fluids via IV and oxygen. I'll put the mask back on in a minute. I also had to strip you to insert a catheter, but I vow that's all I did."

I nodded. "I believe you."

Silence filled the room for a few minutes as I closed my eyes and let my thoughts spin. Reopening them, I looked up at the ragged face of Dr. Maestro.

"What the fuck are we going to do?"

He sighed and scratched at the beard I guessed he didn't normally wear. "Pray, my dear. It's about the only thing we have left to us."

He reached over to put the oxygen mask back over my face, ending our conversation for the moment. I fought back the tears that stung my eyes. They would do no good, only waste energy I was sure I'd need later. Instead, I took the doctor's advice. I closed my eyes and prayed.

Blade

Three days. Veronica had been in Elita's hands for three fucking days.

I paced around the yard of the new house where we were based, unable to stay still. Unable to sleep or eat. I couldn't stop imagining what my woman was going through each moment of the day and night. Was she even still alive?

"Blade!"

Mac's sharp voice cut through my thoughts, bringing me to a halt to look over toward him and the house.

"Come inside. It's time."

Despite the fact most of the wildfires were now out, the air was still tinged with smoke. I took one last, deep breath of the scent before I marched over to follow Mac inside. I was ashamed that I hadn't been a bigger part of planning Veronica's rescue, but from the moment I'd learned she'd been taken, something inside me broke and I'd lost my mind.

Nitro had ended up knocking me out with some pressure point shit, and while I'd been out, the fucker had drugged me to keep me that way. By the time I woke up this morning in this new house I'd never seen before, over half the club was here, including Mac and Scout. While I'd been out, Keys had tracked the bugs he'd put in her shoes and located Elita's stronghold, and they'd formulated a plan. They'd just been waiting on me to wake the fuck up, which I had this morning.

I was still furious with Nitro for knocking me out like he had, but I knew I couldn't take the former SEAL and would only end up injured and unable to participate in Veronica's rescue. But at some point I was going to have it out with the man.

Speaking of the devil, he came straight at me as I entered the rear of the house.

"Blade, we need to talk."

I glared at him. "So talk, but if you even attempt to touch me I will take you down."

We both knew he could beat my ass, but fuck it. If he tried any more shit on me, I'd throw everything in me at having a go at him.

He smirked for a moment before he shook his head. "I did it for your own good, not to hurt you. I knew you'd run off to try to rescue her alone and end up getting you both killed. Blade, you are not on your own anymore. You need to remember that the Charons are not like the mob, we're a family. We take care of our own. I'm sorry I had to do what I did, but it kept you alive, so I don't regret it."

The anger drained from my body at his explanation. I'd been alone for so long, I had no concept of the family bond that ran deep within the Charons. I'd never even considered he'd done it for my and Veronica's safety. I gave him a nod and held out my knuckles for him to bump.

"Forgiven and forgotten, but don't fucking try it again."

With a nod of his own, he turned and I followed him into the front room where at least half the Charons stood, waiting to ride out to rescue my girl. I couldn't help but feel a little choked up at the sight. Most of these men barely knew me.

Mac came to stand in front of me and put a palm on each of my shoulders.

"You are a Charon, Blade. We stand together. Now, let's go get your woman."

Mac and Scout had filled me in on the plan earlier, so there was no need to go over it again. I followed the others outside and got in the van with Bank. The others all had their bikes now, and the roar of Harleys was loud enough to have the van vibrating. I looked in the mirror at the sight behind us and couldn't help but be in awe. The club was all wearing their cuts and the ones at the front who were close enough for me to make out their faces, wore determined expressions. We were doing this. We would prevail.

Hold on, my little dove, we're coming for you.

Bank took off and we headed out of the city toward the hills where Elita's compound was located. The closer we got, the more my muscles grew tense. I had no idea what we'd find when we got there. The club had brought enough weapons with them to start a war, I hoped we wouldn't need them. Innocents tended to get hurt when that much firepower was released. I hated to think we'd find her, only to have her die in the crossfire.

"You love her, don't you?"

Bank was a fairly quiet man and I hadn't spoken with him much. "Yeah. Didn't think I'd ever have a woman of my own. Too risky, you know? But I couldn't help it with Veronica." The fact we were currently driving to her rescue because of me really drove that point home. "I probably should leave her be once we get her free. I can't stand the thought of her suffering again because of me."

"You don't think you leaving her would hurt her? I assure you, that is the worst thing you can do for her if you don't want her hurt."

I shifted my gaze to him, taking in his serious face. "That sounded like you're talking from experience."

He shrugged. "Long time ago now. It's in the past."

"But it made its mark."

He nodded but didn't take his gaze from the road. "That, it did."

We fell into silence after that as we made our way closer to the compound. We were only a few minutes away when I pulled my gun out and checked it was fully loaded and the safety was off.

"How good a shot are you with that?"

I raised an eyebrow at Bank's question. "I've spent a lot of time at the range, and have taken out my share of men over of the years. My aim is good. You?"

I was equally good at throwing knives, but I didn't think the man needed to know that.

"The club has a deal with the range in Bridgewater. Scout makes sure we're all trained. I'm solid. We all are."

"Good to know."

My heart began to race as we came up to the iron gates.

The time to kick some mob ass and save my girl had arrived.

Chapter 9

Veronica

With a pained expression, Dr. Maestro told me it was time to call an end to the ruse. He went over to the door and called out to the guard that I was awake before he returned to me. He set about removing the IV and catheter.

"I truly am sorry I couldn't give you more time. She is an extremely cruel woman and I can only imagine what she intends to put you through."

I looked into his hollow eyes once more. "I'm sorry for both of us. Neither of us deserve this hell we've found ourselves in. Blade will come. The club will come. We just need to hold on."

He gave me a sad smile. "Oh, she'll make sure I survive. She likes having a doctor around to fix up her men who won't ask questions. It's you I worry for. What she had done to Lilly…" he shook his head, clenching his jaw.

Fear had my blood cooling when the door snicked once more and I looked over to see the woman for the first time who was about to make my life hell.

"Ah, so she does, in fact, live. Miss Jones, you've certainly kept me waiting, and deprived me of my favorite toy for days by doing so. I wonder how you can repay me for that…" she trailed off as she strutted toward me.

She was all high-end class. Long, platinum blonde hair that was dead straight, eyes so blue I suspected she wore colored contacts. Her nails were painted a cliché blood red. They were long and shaped into points. Weapons she could take everywhere.

Two men had come in with her and when she flicked her fingers toward Dr. Maestro, they moved to grip his arms, forcing him against a wall where they secured his cuffs to rings screwed into the wall. Elita walked up in front of him and cupped his balls in her palm. "Did my boy miss me these past days?" He shuddered but stayed mute. Bile rose in my throat as she played with him until he hardened for her. "I'll be back to play with you soon." She blew an air kiss before she turned her cold eyes to me. "Strip her."

My blood ran ice cold in my veins as one of men took the edge of the sheet and ripped it off me. I tugged against the cuffs holding me down, trying desperately to break free somehow. I'd been raped enough times to last me ten lifetimes already. I wasn't going to lay down and take it without a fight, no matter how much I ended up hurting myself in the process.

"Hmm, she's got some fight in her. Nice. It's so much more fun to break the strong ones. That last nurse was weak. She broke way too easily. I certainly hope Blade enjoyed finding her."

I paused in my struggling to glare my hatred at her. "You left her body for him to find? Why?"

I was now naked in the cuffs, her man having stepped back to allow her to come up to the side of the table where I lay. She ran a nail down my cheek, scratching me with the sharpened point. I held in the wince at the streak of pain, refusing to let her see she'd hurt me in any way, and knowing worse was soon to come my way.

"So innocent. He didn't tell you what he did? How he turned on the man who took him in as a teen and raised him as his own."

My growl cut her off. "That's not how he tells it."

She laughed and I glimpsed her palm a moment before pain radiated across my face. Her backhand split my lip and filled my mouth with the taste of my own blood.

"I wouldn't recommend interrupting me again. I have a little issue with my temper, especially since your boyfriend murdered my father."

The glint in her eyes had me clenching my jaw. She was fucking insane, completely mentally unstable. This wasn't going to end well. No matter how hard I fought, this was going to hurt. A lot. She stepped back from the table and waved a hand to her men. "Get her up against the wall, I'm going to go get the others. Playtime is here."

I cringed away from the smirks her men wore as they flipped open the cuffs and pulled me from the table. I tried to lash out but I'd been tied down for so long, and was no doubt still recovering from my drug overdose, that my muscles refused to respond like they normally did. In moments, I was cuffed and chained to the wall beside Dr. Maestro, who stood staring blankly into space, as though he'd found a way to disconnect from his body.

Bile rose up my throat when one of the men ran his hand down my front, tweaking a nipple on his way.

"We're gonna have so much fucking fun breaking you, baby. She won't let you die easy, either. Nope, she'll make you suffer so much more than she did that other little bitch, because he claimed you. We're gonna have weeks, maybe even months of fucking all your pretty little holes. Make sure you're well used and utterly ruined, then, maybe she'll return you to him. Let him see what we've done to you."

I swallowed down the bile. Steeled myself against what was about to happen. I knew this bastard was telling me the truth. My life was about to return to being hell, one worse than the one I'd survived already. Before her men could do more to me, a shout from outside the room drew their attention and they both ran for the door. As soon as they left, I tested the cuffs, twisting and turning to see if I could slip free somehow.

"It's pointless. They never leave a way out."

Dr. Maestro's low voice had me pausing for only a second before I kept trying to break free.

"I can't not try."

He gave me a small nod but didn't say anything else as I continued to twist and tug until my wrists burned from the cuffs rubbing against my flesh. Suddenly a loud burst of sounds from the hallway had me stilling.

"Was that—"

"Gunfire. Yes. Perhaps your man has indeed come for you."

"Not just me, us. He was already coming to rescue you when I was taken."

"Right."

He didn't sound like he believed me but I didn't care right then. So long as Blade came through the door in the next few minutes, I didn't care about a damn thing else.

The door snicked once more but what came through was the last thing I expected. Or wanted. A decidedly worse for wear looking Elita was thrust inside. Her clothing was ripped, one eye was bruised and swollen shut, and she had a cut on her cheek that looked like a fist wearing a ring had struck her. She stumbled on her now shoeless feet as she tried to maintain her balance with my uncle shoving her forward again with a gun to her back.

"No. Oh, *fuck no.*"

Ignoring Dr. Maestro's glance at me, I shook my head as I continued to curse under my breath. This couldn't be happening. I couldn't be this unlucky. To go from one hell to another.

"Ah, finally, there you are, my sweet baby girl. You certainly have been hard to pin down."

My whole body trembled violently at my uncle's smooth Texan drawl. It was supposed to be Blade coming to my rescue, not him.

"How did you find me?"

"Your abduction made the news, my dear. Your neighbor saw you being snatched and called in the cavalry. From there it wasn't hard to call in a few favors to find out where you were."

"Favors?"

Several men came in behind my uncle, the largest one grabbing Elita with a firm grip in her hair and shoving her against the wall, shackling her in her own cuffs before he turned to speak to me.

"Yes, favors. Lucky for your uncle, I've wanted to take over from the Sabella family for a long damn time. Antonio wouldn't allow me to marry this one, so now we'll take another path. I bet you're regretting your decision to reject me so harshly now aren't you, Elita? You could have been my queen. Now you'll be my slut before I'll allow you to join your father."

My gaze and attention were torn from her when my uncle stepped up close to me, resting his warm palm over his mark on my hip.

"You still wear my mark. Good."

What choice did I have? He'd fucking tattooed it into my skin. If I could have removed it, I would have long ago. When he leaned in and inhaled against my neck, I once more found myself swallowing down bile. Unable to hold them in any longer, tears streaked down my cheeks. With all my clothes stripped from me, all of Keys' trackers were also gone. I doubted my uncle would let me take any of them from where they sat in the corner. That meant my life was now over. Done. My uncle would make sure I was hidden away so well no one would ever see me again. My lungs would draw in air, my heart would continue to beat, but my soul would soon be gone. I knew it as sure as I knew the sun would rise again in the morning.

"Boss, what do you want to do with this one?"

He leaned back to turn toward the conversation the other men were having. The man still holding Elita against the wall with her hair, looked over at Dr. Maestro, eying his state of undress and the bruises that marred his flesh before he shrugged.

"End his suffering, leave him here."

"No!"

I called out before I could think it through. Every eye in the room turned to me. My uncle took my chin in his fingers so I was forced to look into his cold, hard eyes.

"Why would you have us spare his life?"

"He saved me. When Elita's men took me, they drugged me and gave me an overdose. Dr. Maestro saved my life. Without him, you would have found my dead body today."

Fury flared in his gaze and before I could catch my breath, he pushed away from me and strode over to where

Elita hung from her own shackles. The other man stepped back to allow him access as he watched on with a curious expression.

My uncle's voice was a cold whip. "Not only did you dare touch what is mine, you nearly killed her?"

Watching Elita shake with fear did bring me a spark of pleasure in my own mind-numbing fear. It was short lived, though. My uncle delivered a solid blow to her side, most likely breaking a rib or two before he grabbed her chin in a brutal grip, forcing her to focus on his face.

"I'm a firm believer in vengeance, Ms. Sabella. You had my Victoria stripped bare and no doubt were about to order all manner of things done to her. I can see from the doctor's body that you've done the same to him. It's time for you to get a taste of what you deal out, my dear."

The other man cleared his throat. "That was not our deal, Jovan. You can take the doctor along with your girl, but Elita is mine to punish. You can stay and watch if you'd like, but it'll be me in charge."

I squeezed my eyes shut, tried to close off my hearing. I did not want to witness her rape. No matter how much I hated her for what she'd done to me and Dr. Maestro, I didn't want this for her. Didn't want to hear it or see it.

I jerked when my uncle's palm cupped my cheek. "Sweet baby girl, do you not want to witness her punishment?"

Still refusing to open my eyes, I shook my head no.

"Still so innocent. And what would you have me do with your fellow captive, hmm?"

"Free him. All he did was his job, treated a man Elita didn't like at the hospital where he worked. Nothing more. She's had him for weeks, tortured him. He didn't deserve any of it. Yet he still chose to save my life. He's earned his freedom, Uncle."

With my eyes still closed I didn't see him move but his warm breath heated my ear, making a shiver of revulsion go down my spine. "If you want him spared, you need to pay a price, baby girl. You will come with me willingly. No fighting, no escaping."

More tears left my eyes as deep inside, my soul began to die, just as I knew it would. My uncle would never let me be free. Images of Blade flashed across the inside of my closed lids. Of his smile, of the way his face went lax when he came. The sensation of his hands on my body, loving me. Things I'd never experience again.

I nodded to my uncle. No matter what I said or did from here on out, my life was over. I might as well try to save Dr. Maestro if I could.

"Open your eyes and look at me when you give me your word. I'll not have you lie to me."

I blinked open my eyes and nearly gagged at the sight that greeted me. The other man was standing back with his arms crossed as he instructed his goons, who were tearing at Elita's clothing, pawing her body as they did. Seeing her being prepared had me flashing back to my own rapes at my uncle's hand and a whimper left my throat before I could call it back. Fingers on my chin tilted my face away from the sight and forced my gaze to meet my uncle's. The excitement lighting his eyes made me want to throw up all over again. He was possibly even more insane than Elita.

"Give me your word, Victoria."

I hated my name, but was glad he didn't contaminate my new name by saying it. I would hold on to Blade's voice whispering Veronica in his deep baritone for the rest of my days, untainted by my uncle's voice saying the same name.

"If you spare Dr. Maestro's life, I will come with you willingly and not attempt to escape."

His smile was a cold thing, like how I imagined a snake would grin at its next meal.

"Good, baby. Although, we'll not leave him here. I doubt you want him to be left to be their plaything once they get through with Elita. We'll take him with us and once I have you safely sequestered back where you belong, we'll set him free."

It was the best I could do for the man. I had no clue if my uncle would honor his words, because I sure as fuck didn't intend to honor mine. If I got even half a chance to run from him, I would, promise be damned.

Elita Sabella

After that fucker, Jovan, left with my captives, I could do nothing but hang from my own fucking shackles as I waited for what Makar Smirnov was going to do to me next. He'd already had his men strip me naked, tearing and cutting my clothes from me as I tried to pull free from the cuffs I knew would never give. Thick leather bands enclosed my wrists and ankles that were connected by short chains to rings embedded into the stone wall behind me. I'd held enough prisoners in this room to know there was no escaping. But, ironically, just like my victims, I fought against them anyway.

With a wave of his hand, his men had stepped away from me once I was naked and now he stood staring at me. I kept my chin up and my gaze hard. I refused to allow him to see he affected me at all, even though he always had. My father had been irate at the very thought of a Russian family being involved with the family business and had quickly forbid me from any contact with Makar soon after his arrival in L.A.

It wasn't until much later that I'd learned about all of Makar's attempts to have my father betroth me to him. As though this was the eighteenth century or something, and I was my father's property to give away at his pleasure. I'd never had any intention of taking a man permanently. Never had any desire to reproduce.

As Makar set about calmly removing his jacket and cufflinks, then started in on slowly rolling up his sleeves, my mind swirled with questions and recriminations. How had this happened? My father had taught me well. As he'd trained me to do, I'd groomed my closest guards carefully to be one-hundred percent loyal to me. They'd witnessed the price if they weren't. I'd been a harsh boss, but they were rewarded richly for their service to me. When I'd sent Nicolas to follow Blade and report back, I'd thought I'd hit the jackpot when the stupid bastard had taken on a girlfriend. He should have just headed to Mexico and hidden under a rock for the next ten years. That's what I would have done in his position. In my excitement of finding such a big weakness, I hadn't done due diligence on researching her past. I had no fucking clue that his little Veronica Jones was really the missing Victoria Jovan, niece and apparently plaything to the mayor of Greenswood, Allen Jovan, who was best friends with none other than the man who'd been desperate to make me his for the past decade.

I'd heard about Jovan years ago, when his niece first went missing. He'd called in favors back then too, but no one had been able to find any information on where the girl had disappeared to. I'd had no clue that she'd stayed hidden all this time.

"Elita, *malysh*, at last, you're all mine."

I growled when he stepped up and pressed his hard body against mine, pinning me against the wall so I couldn't move at all.

"Now, now. Don't be like that." He reached up and wrapped his palm around my breast, squeezing it hard enough to make my eyes water before he gave my nipple a hard tug.

"Such a pity you and your father chose this path for us, *malysh*. I spoke the truth earlier. I would have made you my queen. We could have ruled this city together. But instead your father disrespected me, told me I wasn't good enough for his precious Elita." He leaned in and bit at my jaw, hard. I clenched my teeth so the whimper didn't leave me. "You didn't think I was good enough either, did you?"

I couldn't help but respond. "Don't take it so personally, Makar, I didn't want any man."

He laughed darkly. "Looked like you wanted and had that doctor a number of times, so don't bullshit me. Since I'm clearly not good enough for you, let's see if I'm bad enough, *da*?"

When he turned to his men and instructed them to go get his ropes, fear like I'd never known had my limbs trembling against my will.

He stroked his knuckles down my cheek while he waited for his men to return.

"Such soft skin. But that's the only soft part of you, *da*? I had plans for us. Children, big house… but you never would have wanted any of that, would you? You truly are as stone-cold as your father told me you were. You would make a terrible leader. You need some compassion, some level of care for those who come under the umbrella of your protection. You have none for anyone other than yourself. Let's see if we can teach you a little humility to take into your next life, *da*?"

He pressed a soft kiss to my cheek before turning to take the bundle of rope from his man. My heartbeat thundered in my ears as, in silence, he shifted my ankle cuff to be locked to a higher ring, then he tied my knee to my elbow, which left my pussy wide open for him. His gaze lit up and his two men standing behind him took their cocks out and started stroking themselves as Makar pulled his belt free. But he didn't undo his fly next, like I expected. No, it was worse. He folded that thick leather in two and raised it high before swinging it down against my inner thigh.

My world became a blur of pain and humiliation. I had no idea how long Makar and his men kept at me but when they finally had enough, they left me hanging in my own dungeon. Makar's parting words, telling me to enjoy dying a slow, painful death and I could say hello to my father in hell when I finally joined him, rang in my ears as I screamed into the now empty room.

Slowly, my mind managed to push through the pain and thoughts began to swirl again. Not that it did me any good. I was still chained in my own unescapable cuffs, only now I didn't have the energy to even attempt to fight free of them. My entire body ached, inside and out. I'd be impressed, if I hadn't been the recipient of the abuse. Rage heated my blood. Anger at myself, Makar, Blade and my father twisted inside me until my body vibrated with it.

The one goal that had motivated me since my father's death would go unattained. I would die in this room, from either whatever internal injuries I had sustained, or dehydration and starvation, while his murderer was still free. At least I could die knowing that Blade would never find his precious Veronica. Jovan would lock that girl away so well, she wouldn't even see daylight, let alone other people. That would have to be enough. Knowing that Blade would suffer the rest of his life not having any idea what his woman was suffering through. Being unable to save her.

I would go unsaved too. All my men who knew about this location were here when Makar and Allen stormed my walls and were all now slaughtered. The only others who knew this property existed were my brother and mother, but neither of them would be coming any time soon. No, those worthless, spineless pussies had run as soon as we'd gotten word of father's death. They'd seen their freedom and fled, while I'd seen a need to avenge his death and track down his murderer. My father had figured out early on that his son would never be a made man, but he'd seen it in me. Seen that I was more than capable, and even though I was a girl, he'd groomed me to one day take over for him.

And what a fine job I'd done of that.

"Fuck!"

I cursed loudly, the sound echoing around the room. I'd been the head of the family for less than a month and I'd fucked up and got myself brutalized and left for dead. Makar telling me I would never have made a good leader had me growling again. If I somehow managed to get free from here, Makar Smirnov and Allen Jovan both would pay dearly for what they'd done here today.

"Whoa." A large man wearing a leather vest skidded to a halt in the doorway, taking in my bloody and battered body for a silent minute before he turned and called down the hallway. "Found her!"

What sounded like an army came running toward us. I had no clue who this man was, and from the front of his vest, I couldn't tell what club he was affiliated with. A fragile flicker of hope formed within me that maybe I was saved. Until the next man entered. I sighed out a heavy breath but, despite my head wanting to fall forward on my neck, I refused to lower my gaze as Blade, my father's killer, entered the room.

"What the fuck, man? Don't say you found her, when you know this isn't the fucking *her* I'm looking for!"

The other man shrugged with a wince. "Sorry, Blade. Didn't think, seeing her like this was a shock."

Blade strode over to me as a dozen others came in behind him. This small room was suddenly very crowded.

"Where the fuck is she?"

I clenched my jaw tightly shut. I would say nothing to help this murderer. He waved a hand up and down, indicating my body.

"Why the fuck would you protect the ones who did this to you?"

I turned my glare on him, staring him in the eye, enjoying the pain I saw there. "Because you murdered my father, the man who took you in, took care of you, treated you like a fucking son!"

He shook his head. "I can't believe you of all people don't know the truth of what I was to your father. I was nothing more than a possession, like any of his weapons. I was never a son to him, he never *took* me in. My father sold me to him when I was sixteen to pay off a protection debt that he owed to your family. From there Antonio had me trained to be the killing machine he needed me to be, but he never could break me completely. That drove him nuts. Drove him to torment me with Josefina."

I rolled my eyes, breaking eye contact with him. "That little piece of fluff was nothing to anyone. A little *puta* from across the border who caught my father's eye."

Blade's palm stung as it connected with my cheek, causing my head to snap to the side and back against the wall with a thunk. I was surprised the pain registered when my head connected with the stone, considering the throbbing pain I felt from everywhere else on my body.

"Do not *ever* speak of her that way again. She was a sister to me and your father took her away and abused her for decades for no reason other than to hurt me. Your father was evil, the devil himself, and he did a great job in creating you in his image." He paused and took a step back to stand directly in front of me, arms folded over his chest. Just as Makar had done before he'd begun his torture. "Last chance to do this the easy way, Elita. Who took her?"

I tilted my chin up, ignoring the throbbing in my head the smack against the wall had caused.

"Have it your way. Did Antonio ever tell you why they call me Blade?"

Somehow I managed to keep my expression blank, but my heart rate took off once more, beating so hard I wondered if it might burst within me. Wishing it would, as I was quite certain that would be an easier death than the one Blade would deliver. Because, of course, I knew how he'd earned his name. My father had shown me what all of his men were capable of as part of my grooming.

He'd actually warned me never to cross Blade. That no matter what I might think I had to leverage against him, nothing would sway him. My father had attempted to break this man, but instead had created a monster he couldn't control. I had forgotten that conversation when I'd planned out my vengeance upon him for killing my father. I'd been blinded by my grief and would now pay the ultimate price for my stupidity and ignorance.

My second, and I suspected my final, mistake. First was not fully investigating Veronica Jones' past, now I'd underestimated my target. The results of the first had left me vulnerable to suffer the second.

My gaze stayed glued to Blade as he flipped the safety on his gun and holstered it before he reached for his pocket. He removed a closed switch blade. The grin on his face was enough for my false smile to falter. No one could hold their composure when faced with such a chillingly evil grin.

"Let's play, shall we?"

Two of the other men came at me, releasing me from the wall and moving me to the table where I'd had Veronica strapped down such a short time ago. Makar had worked me over front and back with his belt and I bit my tongue to not cry out as my already battered body hit the cold metal. I kept my gaze on Blade, on his crazy fucking eyes. Hopefully he'd lose himself to his insanity and end me quickly. I knew, no matter what, I wasn't going to leave this room alive.

I'd sealed my fate with two simple mistakes.

My father would be rolling over in his grave at the mess I'd created for myself.

Blade

I'd morphed into my other half. The monster Antonio had created so long ago. Normally, I was extremely careful to keep my inner beast chained at all times. These past few days had been a constant struggle to keep it from rising up and destroying everything near me. What no one knew was, it scared me as much as it scared my targets, but there were times I needed that monster. Times like this. Someone had come and destroyed Elita's world, burned her fledging empire to the ground before it had a chance to take off. And they'd taken my woman with them.

For Veronica, I'd allow the beast within to fly free and play. I knew Mac would help me rein it in once I was done. For now I allowed my entire focus to be on the fact that Elita had information I needed. Mac and Machete had pulled her from the wall and restrained her to the table before stepping away. I could hear the murmur of their voices. Mac was the only one here who knew what lived inside me. None of the other Charons had any fucking idea about this side of me. I could only assume Mac was sharing a few details, but I couldn't focus on them. Elita had my full attention. Her eyes were bright blue, and the fact they were still that fake color meant her contacts were intact and she would be able to see clearly everything I was about to do to her. She swallowed as she continued to stare at me. She'd dropped her tough facade the moment I'd pulled my switch blade out, and now she was nothing but a mess of weakness. My gaze ran down her body, cataloging the damage already done to her. She'd been struck numerous times with what I guessed was a belt from the width of the welts covering her. There were several bite marks along her jaw and collarbones, bruising was clear to see among the red welts over her chest and down her torso. Blood slicked her inner thighs, over more welts, and had trailed down to her feet. Whoever had come to take her down had beaten and raped her, brutally. I would need to be careful as to not kill her before she revealed the information I needed. My instincts told me she was close to death already.

"Not so tough now, are we Elita? No Daddy to come save you, no army of blackmailed men to do your bidding. You're all alone."

I hit the button and my blade flew open with a small sound. A sound that had my target flinching against her bonds and making me grin.

"Your daddy told you about me, didn't he? Yet you still decided to come after me. Well, bitch, here I am. You have my full fucking attention, just like you wanted."

Ignoring everyone else in the room, I wrapped my hand around her foot, holding it still for me to make a small slice into the tender skin of the arch with my sharp blade. Her body tensed and I grinned at her attempt to remain stoic. Whoever had come before us had already broken her down to her limit, it wouldn't take much to have her spilling all sorts of secrets.

After I made the fifth cut, I paused and shifted my gaze from her bleeding feet to her eyes and decided to start with something not about Veronica.

"Where are your brother and mother? Do they know about your plan?"

She shook her head as she panted through the pain for a few moments. "They ran the second we heard of father's death. Pussies."

"So your brother has no desire to take over the family business then?"

I needed to know, because if he did, I'd go take him out as soon as I had Veronica safe. No more loose ends.

She grinned wide, falsely, and refused to answer, so I moved up her legs, delivering more of the painful but non-lethal cuts to the backs of her knees with the precision that had caused Antonio to start calling me Blade. With a rough grip on her knee, I shoved it out as far as I could so I could start slicing my way up her inner thigh. Her skin was slick with her blood and the welts showed her previous attacker must have restrained her legs open to reach all her most sensitive areas with his belt before he fucked her.

I'd known so many men who were so quick to use rape as a tool to hurt a woman, but I'd never once even considered it. The act ran against every moral instinct I had. Physical pain was one thing, but sexual pain was a whole other level in which I would never participate. But it didn't mean I wouldn't use the threat of it to help me to get the bitch to talk.

Skipping over her thighs that were already beaten enough I knew she wouldn't even feel any cuts I made, I trailed the tip of my blade from one hip bone to the other, not enough to draw blood but the threat was clear.

"Your brother?"

Her body trembled and moisture welled in her eyes as I lightly scraped the tip of my blade over her mound, not that I gave a fuck she was upset.

"He's soft. Too soft for this life. He has no interest in it. He's studying architecture. He's no threat to you. Nor is my mother."

Her words were rushed and I nearly didn't catch everything she said. I stepped back, removing the knife from her most delicate skin. But I didn't give her long to catch her breath before I moved to hold her hand, forcing her fingers to splay out to reveal her palm. With the tip once more posed to break skin, I paused and holding her gaze asked again.

"Who came before us? Who has Veronica?"

Her jaw clenched and I pressed the blade down, entering the center of her palm slowly.

She spoke through clenched teeth, but I still heard her every word. "Don't you mean Victoria?"

The beast rose to the surface, snarling, and Elita's eyes went wide as she held my gaze before I started speaking.

"You're reckless and impulsive. So I doubt you personally looked into Veronica's past enough to know about her real name. That means her uncle was here, but unlike you, I've done my fucking research and know that there's no fucking way he did this alone. Who fucking took my woman, Elita?"

Fury lit me up as the bitch stayed silent and in my rage, I stepped up my routine. No more small cuts. I tossed my switch blade onto the table, and she flinched as it clattered against the metal. Ripping open the holster that held my fixed blade hunting knife, I pulled it free and held her fingers out flat. After lining my blade up with the bottom joint of her pinky finger, I made fast work of removing the digit, ignoring her screams as I grabbed some shredded material off the floor and wrapped the bleeding stub.

"Here, use this."

Machete handed me a roll of duct tape and tossing the material aside, I tore off a strip. She screamed again as I roughly sealed the wound enough she wouldn't bleed out before I wanted her to, but I barely heard her as I imagined what Veronica was suffering through right now. Her uncle had come and taken her. Her uncle who had proven how much he liked to hurt her, had her. Fuck. Not only that, but another player was involved. Whoever it was could be with Jovan taking payment from my girl, or the doctor. We hadn't found any sign of him yet, either.

"What about the doctor? Did they take him too?"

Aside from her panting through clenched teeth, she remained mute. I was past done with her bullshit. I moved until I was staring directly into her face, then holding her jaw in my fingers, I rested the bloody knife against her cheek, pressing the tip against the skin below her eye.

"I'm about out of patience, bitch, and you have plenty of other body parts I can chop off. So, stop fucking around, and answer my fucking questions. What happened to the doctor?"

Her breaths stuttered and when I felt the muscles of her jaw flex, I loosened my grip to allow her to speak.

"Jovan took them both. Your woman promised compliance if they let the doctor go. Although I highly doubt they will honor that promise. You know who she is to him, right? He'll never release her, he'll hide her away from the world now. She'll never even see the sun again, let alone you."

I leaned over her, getting my face close to hers so she could see the fury and determination in my gaze. She stopped talking and a shiver racked through her body as I dragged the tip down her cheek, making a shallow cut.

"You should have left me and mine alone. Your father got what he deserved. You know that. You should have just taken the windfall it gave you and enjoyed it, but no.

You had to come after me. And now that you're caught in your own fucking trap, you still insist on trying to hurt me with empty words. I know exactly who my woman is to that fucker. I'm not mob anymore, princess. I'm Charon MC and we have friends, ones who know exactly where Allen Jovan lives and plays. Need to know who else I need to chase down, so who the fuck helped Jovan?"

Her eyes flared with hatred. Interesting. She hated whoever had helped Jovan even more than she did me. That was saying something.

"Fucking tell me! Or you lose another finger."

I turned back toward her hand and switched my grip on my knife, ready to take another digit off.

"Smirnov!"

I paused and turned back to frown down at her. "Makar Smirnov?"

The big Russian bastard had hung around Sabella years ago, trying to get in good with the man. I'd thought he'd returned to Russia after Antonio shut him down.

"Yes. He wanted control of L.A., and—" she paused and snarled before finishing, "and of me. Father denied him both, so he used Jovan's request for a favor to get what he wanted. He doesn't give a shit about your woman or the doctor."

Her voice had weakened as she'd spoken. She was resigned to her fate and no longer gave a fuck about withholding information from me. Her words helped me understand the condition her body was in. I could easily see Makar getting his vengeance on the Sabella family by torturing Elita as he had. I'd also bet he planned on returning in a day or so to torture her some more before taking her with him. He'd either keep her as his own personal whore or sell her off to be used as one. All things considered, she should be thanking me for what I was about to do. Because there was no way in hell I would allow this bitch to breathe air in a world where my Veronica lived.

"All of this could have been prevented, Elita. None of this was fucking necessary. None of it. But you started this shit, so I'm finishing it. Just know, it will take me less than a day to have Veronica back in my arms, where she belongs. While you will be lying here dead with no one left who cares enough to even mourn your loss. Enjoy hell, bitch."

With that I lifted up and delivered the final slice, deep across her throat. I stood there, staring into her eyes as she gasped her final breath, then taking both my knives I turned and walked away from her. Pausing briefly on my way out of the room to pick up some of her discarded clothing to wipe my blades clean. I'd clean them with bleach later, but for now I just put them away.

"We need to head back to Texas. Her uncle has her and the doctor. I'll get Keys to keep an eye on Smirnov, but I can't see him worrying about us now he has what he wants."

I was sure he'd be angry when he found Elita dead, but he'd wanted control of the mob more than her so I was fairly certain he wouldn't give me another thought.

Mac came to walk beside me. "You didn't let the prez do his usual spiel, Blade."

I gave him a fast glare before I focused back on where I was walking. While I appreciated that he was just trying to get me out of beast mode with some humor, until I had Veronica back, it wouldn't work.

"Scout likes to explain how the Charons are named after the Greek ferryman who would decide if souls went to Hades or the Elysian Fields—"

"Mac?"

"Yeah?"

"Shut the fuck up, brother."

"Right."

I really didn't give a fuck that Scout normally liked to play with his victims, fuck with their minds. Personally, I think I did a fine job of messing with Elita's head before

I took her out. I got to the van and opened the door to get in, wishing I had my bike here. My beast was out and didn't want to be caged.

"Blade! Hold up a sec."

I paused before I slid into the seat to turn to face Scout. I'd thought Mac had been joking but now was wondering if the club president would really be mad that I'd killed Elita before he could do his thing. I opened my mouth to apologize but he waved it off.

"Don't worry about that, Mac was just trying to lighten the mood. You did just fine. Fucking scary as hell, but got the job done. What I want to tell you is that we're heading back to Bridgewater first. Some of the Satan's Cowboys are coming down to meet with us to plan how to deal with Jovan."

I shook my head. No fucking way.

"I can't wait, Scout. He won't. He'll rape her as soon as he can. He started grooming her basically from birth. He made her life a living hell, when her folks sent her away to boarding school to try to save her. He'd had them killed to get her back. His own brother and his wife." I shook my head again. "I can't sit on this." I gestured to the mess around us. "We're only a few hours behind them. We ride to Greenswood and take them down before they can get settled anywhere. Before he can get her locked away."

Scout stood with his fists against his hips, glaring at me but his silence indicated he heard what I'd said, that he was thinking it through. With a curse, he sighed before he pulled his phone out.

"Hey, Viper, Scout here. Looks like there's a change of plans. We're coming to you."

He continued speaking into his phone but I didn't track the words, relief that he wasn't going to force me to go back to Bridgewater and sit on my fucking hands while Veronica was being abused flowed through me. The Cowboys were located in Cutler, only about a twenty minute drive away from where Allen had his home. I liked the idea of having another entire club to back us up when we rode in. It also helped that, despite the Cowboys being a one percenter club, they were firmly against human trafficking of any kind. And holding a woman against her will as a sexual slave fell under that category.

Hold on, little dove. I'm coming for you.

Chapter 10

Veronica

My uncle had forced his men to drive without stopping for anything more than gas, food and bathroom breaks. The upside to this was it hadn't given him time to start mauling me yet. Although I knew that time was limited as the convoy of cars passed through the gates at the edge of his property and delivered me right back to the hell I'd tried so hard to escape.

"Remember your promise, baby."

I loathed that endearment. He'd always used it on me. Baby girl, sweet baby or simply baby, like he'd called me just now. It made me want to punch something every time I heard it. But I knew any attempt at violence wouldn't end well for me right now, so I breathed away the anger and tried to focus on a memory of Blade calling me his little dove.

Dr. Maestro sat rigid beside me. He was now wearing a pair of pants that were way too big for him, while I was wearing nothing but a men's button up shirt. Apparently Uncle Allen didn't think to bring spare clothing for me, much less for the doctor. One of his men had offered up his spare change of clothes, thankfully, so neither of had to sit here for the long drive buck-ass naked.

The car rolled to a stop and after Uncle Allen stepped free of the vehicle, he turned and held his hand out for me to take so he could help me from the car. I hated to touch him at all, but knew it was easier to give in on something as trivial as touching his hand. But I released the hold as soon as I could, wrapping my arms around my waist. Once we were a few feet from the car, I turned to see Dr. Maestro slowly following us as we headed toward the house. My feet were bare and I was grateful for the freshly swept, paved path. I focused on each of the carefully laid stones as we moved closer to the house. My prison. By the time we reached the door, my body trembled as the ball of dread in my stomach grew bigger. This was it. I glanced around quickly, taking in the trees, grass, even the sleek, black cars sitting in the driveway. I took deep breaths of the air. Unlike L.A., there was no smoke in it here. Just clean, country air.

"Come, Victoria."

His sharp voice had me stepping through the door for what I suspected would be the last time. The thud of it closing behind me echoed through me like a church bell. Dr. Maestro came to stand close to my side, close enough I could feel his body heat. Staff came running toward us when my uncle called out to them.

"Take him to a guest room. He'll need clean clothes. Do not let him leave."

I glanced over to the doctor's face. His features were stony and I had no clue what to tell him. He'd heard me barter for his freedom, a freedom my uncle was already denying. But I knew better than to call him on it in front of his staff. I'd ask later when it was just the two of us, to see if I could convince him to let the man go. He really hadn't deserved the hell he'd already suffered, let alone what he'd suffer here under my uncle's hand.

Since I was looking in another direction, watching Dr. Maestro be led away, I didn't see what my uncle intended to do until it was too late to brace against it. In quick movements, he wrapped his hands around my biceps in a harsh grip before he thrust me toward two waiting guards.

"Take her to her room. Make sure the windows and doors are guarded at all times." One of his lackeys wrapped his hand around my wrist, shackling me. My uncle's fingers on my chin forced me to look back at him.

"You will clean yourself. I want every speck of dirt removed from your body, do you understand?"

I didn't bother giving him a verbal answer, just nodded and followed the men as they led me away from the entrance. They stayed silent as they led me through the house and up a flight of stairs. Of course he'd put me in a room on the top floor. He probably thought the higher drop from the window would stop me from using it as an exit. I didn't care if I broke both my legs jumping from the thing, as soon as the doctor was free, I intended to try it.

We came to a closed door and the guard not holding me moved to slide a key into the lock and opened the door.

"The bathroom and closet have been stocked for you. Meals will be delivered to you."

His voice was deep and void of all emotion. I didn't even attempt to try to talk him into setting me free. I knew it would be fruitless, and no doubt he'd report the attempt to my uncle and I'd pay for it later. The moment the other guard released my wrist, I stepped through the door. Before I could take a full breath, it was closed behind me and I heard the lock click. Closing my eyes, I let my tears fall.

This was it. These four walls were now my life.

Swiping the tears away, I looked around the room. It wasn't the one I'd stayed in before my escape. This one was fancier, as though my uncle thought if he gilded my cage enough, I wouldn't notice it was still a cage. The four poster bed looked soft and inviting, and since I had barely slept in the car and was still coming off whatever drugs Elita's man had pumped me full of, I was ready to sleep for a damn week. Not that my uncle would allow me that luxury. No doubt I'd only have an hour, maybe two before he came storming in here expecting me to be open to his attentions. Damn, but I hoped he came alone. What he'd do to me was bad enough, but to have witnesses? Others join in at his request would be more than I could handle today. If he did that, it would utterly destroy my soul in minutes. Leave nothing left within me. I knew it would happen at some point, but I just prayed it wouldn't be today.

With a heavy sigh, I went to the dresser and opened drawers until I found underwear, a t-shirt and leggings. Then I went into the bathroom and winced when I caught a glimpse of myself in the mirror. I looked like I felt. Fucking terrible. I flipped the shower on to warm up while I stripped out of the shirt. I opened the cupboard and pulled out new bottles of shampoo, conditioner and body wash. All the exact same as I'd used as a teenager.

Memories of my youth assailed me and nearly sent me to my knees. I forced myself to enter the cubicle and step under the warm flow of water. As I washed myself clean, I watched the dirt swirl and go down the drain, feeling as though each speck of dirt was a piece of me being washed away.

Blade

Despite the fact we'd only stopped when absolutely necessary, we hadn't caught up with Jovan and his crew before we had to turn off toward the Cowboys' clubhouse. Their president stood with his arms crossed as we all pulled up in front of the former hotel.

"Evening, men. Welcome to the Satan's Cowboys clubhouse. Make yourself at home, grab a shower, clean up. Help yourselves to coffee and food in the kitchen. We'll meet in church in an hour."

With that, he turned and headed inside, leaving us to decide whether to follow him in or not. I didn't want to wait five minutes, let alone a fucking hour. What would happen to Veronica in that time? Mac appeared at my side and with a firm grip on my arm, led me inside. He didn't release his hold until he had me up a flight of stairs and into one of the bedrooms.

"I know you want to go now, but we have to wait."

I shook my head, how could he understand? "I can't—"

"Zara has been taken twice from me, and held at gunpoint on a third occasion. Trust me, brother. I get it. But you can't just run in there on a fucking suicide mission. Think, Blade. Jovan has an entire crew backing him up. If we're going to get your woman out of there alive, we need to go in with a plan."

Unable to stay still, I began to pace around the room. I heard what he was saying. Knew he was right. Didn't mean I had to like it.

"Still hate all this fucking waiting. He's not going to hold off on hurting her."

Mac rested against the wall, folding his arms over his chest. "I think he will for a few hours, at least. He had to get back to his compound, then arrange his men to keep the property guarded. I'd also guess he'd want her cleaned up before he'd touch her. That all gives us some time. But even if I'm wrong and he's already gone after her, tell me what's worse—him touching her once before we go in and end him, or running in and getting yourself killed, which will leave him open to abusing her for the rest of her life. That's the choice here."

I growled and clenched my fists, wanting to hit something, someone, but having nothing in front of me to vent on.

"Helluva fucking choice, Mac."

He gave me a solemn nod. "I agree. Neither option is ideal, but you know life rarely presents us with the perfect solution. We gotta make the most of what we have. And in this case, you've hit the fucking jackpot on that one. You got two MCs ready to ride to help you get her back. Scout called Viper as soon as Keys told us about the connection between Jovan and Veronica. Didn't take long for the Cowboys to work out what a fucking bastard he was and that he needed to be taken out. They'd already started working on a plan to take the fucker out before he took Veronica. We've got this. Before the sun rises, you'll have her back in your arms."

A flash of the Josefina taking her last breath in my arms had my knees weakening and I crumpled to the floor.

"She's not Josefina, brother. Veronica's strong, a fighter. And her uncle doesn't want her dead. He wants to possess her, not kill her. We'll get you both through this."

Staring at my hands, I couldn't respond to him. All I could see was the memory of Josefina's blood on my hands. I was toxic to the women I cared for.

Ignoring what Bank had told me earlier, I knew what I had to do.

"After we get her back, I have to let her go."

"What the fuck? Blade, cut the shit." Mac's boots stomped closer to me until I saw them past my hands. "Stand up and look me in the eye. Right fucking now."

He was using a commanding tone that I suspected he'd developed during his time in the USMC, and it was compelling enough I was on my feet before I'd made the decision to follow the order. His eyes were blazing with fury and I clenched my jaw against what he was about to say.

"I'm here in this room not only because it's my fucking job as the Charon's VP, but because we're friends. And as your friend, I'm telling you to not be stupid. You and Veronica both got some seriously fucked-up shit in your past, but you've only known each other for less than a month. Give it a chance. You might not be meant to spend your lives together, but what if you are? What if Veronica is the one who is supposed to smooth out your rough edges? And you're the one who's meant to show her she's safe enough to put down some fucking roots and live a little? You wanna throw away all of that because your past came back and bit you both in the ass? Hate to tell you, Blade, but right now, it's *her* past that's causing the drama, not yours. With Elita dead and her brother not wanting to take over, your past is done. By the time we finish in Greenswood, her past is gonna be dead and buried too. So what the fuck are you running from, exactly?"

With my hands on my hips, I glared at Mac. "You've been spending too much time with Arrow."

His face broke into a grin, which just pissed me off even more. He slapped me on the shoulder as he moved toward the door. "Take a shower and try to relax a little, Blade. I'll go grab your bag and bring it up."

I watched him leave, not moving until the door closed behind him. Then with a heavy sigh, I scrubbed my palms over my face.

"Fuck!"

This was a mess, but Mac was right. There was nothing I could do at the moment, other than get myself as prepared as possible to go in and rescue my woman when the time came. With that thought in mind, I headed to the bathroom, stripped and hit the shower. All the while I cleaned the grime and dirt from the past two day's trials, I planned my strategy, each slice I'd deliver to

Allen Jovan to get the retribution he deserved for touching what was mine. A bullet was too kind for him.

It was an hour and a half later that I was once more getting into the passenger seat of the van beside Bank. We'd finished up in church. I'd been silent as I'd listened to the Cowboys lay out the plan they'd formulated. Scout and Mac made some suggestions and things got finalized. Now we were ready to ride. All told, nearly fifty men were riding up to Jovan's property. There would be no surprise attack with that many bikes rolling in, so the vans were going in first. We had ours and the Cowboys were taking one of theirs. Keys and Donna were on their way from Bridgewater with the Charon's ambulance as well, and would head straight for Jovan's.

I prayed we didn't need it.

It was a silent trip as we drove the short distance from Cutler to Greenswood. Jovan had a large spread on the outskirts of town and we made our way to the road that curved behind the property, pulling in behind a grove of trees.

"Remember, no engaging with anyone until the others get here."

I gave Bank a nod, but we both knew if I saw Veronica being compromised in any way, I was going to jump in and end that shit, plan be damned. Bank shook his head, clearly reading my intentions.

"Let's go."

At my words, we both jogged over to the old fence. Thanks to the rusted barb wire strands no longer being pulled tight, when Bank cut each one, they fell useless to the ground rather than flying back in our faces. With what the Cowboys had found out, we knew Jovan didn't have his guards patrol this back fence line so the downed fence wouldn't get noticed anytime soon. A pretty big oversight on his part, but one we were more than happy to take advantage of.

Once through the fence, we stayed low and ran up to the side of the house. The Cowboys in the other van were doing the same thing from the other side. Both our jobs were to get inside undetected, so when the rest of the rescue team arrived, and the guards headed out the front to meet them, we could grab Veronica and the doctor and get the fuck out of there with them. Whoever didn't have their hands full with them would help the others take out all of Jovan's men. That was going to be the hard part. I wanted it to be my fucking blade that killed the miserable fuck, but if I had Veronica to protect, that would take priority.

With the anticipated body count, we'd decided it was too many to take to the farm to bury so the plan was to load them all into the house and light it up. The authorities would find them, but wouldn't be able to find enough evidence to do much about it. Hell, considering the shit he got up to and how many people he'd been blackmailing, the cops would probably have a fucking party the asshole was finally gone from their town. Not that I cared. All I cared about right now was getting to Veronica and getting her the hell away from here.

Just as the Cowboys had told us, there were no guards patrolling the perimeter of the yard, however, the man standing beneath a barred window nursing what looked like an AK 47 was new. Had to wonder if that was how Jovan knew Smirnov. It would surprise me if the Russian was an arms dealer.

"Guessing we found where he's keeping her."

I nodded at Bank's whispered words and tried to work out how the fuck I was going to be able to take out the guard. He wasn't moving around, just standing stationary. I glanced up above him at the only window on this side of the house that had bars over it. It had to be where Veronica was being held. Jovan wouldn't really give a fuck if the doctor got away now that he had Veronica under lock and key. Time was ticking down but

I still couldn't figure out how to take him out. Shooting the fucker would make too much noise since we didn't have silencers on our weapons. I could throw a knife and kill him. I was well practiced at taking out a man like that, but the chance of him squeezing the trigger as he died was high and the sound would give us away.

The rumble of Harleys became a low drone of sound and had the guard facing toward the front of the house. I held my breath, hoping he'd leave his position. I blew the breath out when he did just that. After readjusting his weapon, he strode toward the front of the house. He didn't go out of view, but he was facing forward and focused away from us. Making the most of the distraction, we bolted for the rear of the house and slipped up to a window beside a large tree that would hopefully keep us from the guard's view long enough for us to get inside.

A fast glance inside showed an unoccupied sitting room, conveniently with a carpeted floor and no furniture sitting beneath the window. Pulling the glass cutter from my pocket, I scored a circle near the bottom of the window and knocked the piece until it tumbled silently to the carpet. Then I quickly reached in and flipped the latch, sliding the window up so we could enter. Most of the house was dark, which made it easy to stick to the shadows as Bank followed me through the first floor to a rear staircase. No doubt, back in the day, this part of the house would have been for the servants, who wouldn't have been allowed to use the main staircase at the front of the home. I was extremely grateful the Cowboys had managed to get hold of blueprints for the house so I knew, roughly, how to get to the room behind that barred window.

Keeping my steps light, I jogged down the darkened hallway, slowing when I saw a guard leaning against a wall beside a closed door. He also had a semi-automatic but wasn't on alert. He had his gun leaning against the wall and had his phone out. His full attention was on the screen that lit up his face in the dark. Pulling out a throwing knife, I took a moment to aim before I let it fly. It embedded deeply into his throat and he dropped his phone to grab his neck but it was too late. I knew where to hit to make death fast and he was seconds away from taking his last breath.

I shoved him away from the doorway he'd fallen in front of and tested the handle. It was locked, and after a quick glance at the dead body, I decided it would be easier to just break the door down. The rumble of the bikes was louder now and I knew the rest of the men were close. Once Jovan realized they were coming for him, he'd most likely come for Veronica. That was why we'd been sent in early, to make sure that didn't happen.

With that thought in mind, I stepped back and placed a solid kick to the door, slamming the timber panel hard enough the lock gave way and the door busted in.

Veronica

The rumble was getting louder. I looked out the window to see the clear night sky. No storm meant that noise was bikes, not thunder. And to be that loud, there had to be a lot of them. I started to chew on my lower lip but stopped when pain from a split fired up. Dare I allow myself hope that was Blade and his club coming to get me? A noise from outside the door had me spinning to look in that direction. Another thump and I was back across the room, grabbing the lamp from beside my bed. Pulling the cord from the outlet, I stood waiting to see who was about to come into the room. If it was my uncle or one of his men trying to get a piece of me, I was going to take a swing and run.

Suddenly the door splintered and flew open. I raised my weapon, ready to swing, when I saw who'd burst through the door. Dropping the heavy lamp, I sobbed and threw myself at Blade, wrapping my arms and legs around him as he wound an arm around my waist, keeping me tight against him while he pressed a kiss to my temple.

"I got you, little dove."

"Let's head back out."

I tensed at the new voice and glanced up, but relaxed when I saw he was wearing a Charon MC vest like Blade's. I buried my face in against his neck, inhaling his scent deep in my lungs. He'd come for me.

"Anything you wanna take, Veronica? We'll be burning this place to the ground by the time we're through."

I shook my head. "There's nothing of mine here. Please, Blade, just get me out of here." I gasped as I remembered the doctor. "We need to find Dr. Maestro before we go!"

With a palm to the back of my head, he pressed my cheek to his shoulder. "Shh, little dove. There's another team looking for him."

Then he started moving. I held tight as we headed to the rear of the house. Once down the stairs he tapped my thigh, indicating I needed to stand. Reluctantly, I released my hold on my savior and stood beside him. He leaned in to speak near my ear.

"There was a guard below your window. Let me take him out, then we'll be running to the rear fence, okay?"

"I don't have shoes."

"I'll carry you—"

Before he could say anything more, shouts filled the night. The roar of Harleys that been growing steadily louder suddenly cut off and fear had me taking a fistful of Blade's shirt over his heart. He took my face between his palms and held my gaze with his.

"Both the Charons and Satan's Cowboys are here for you and the doctor. Anyone wearing a cut—a leather vest—is on your side and can be trusted, understand?"

I nodded. Movement caught my eye and I jerked at the sight of a big man coming out of the shadows behind us. Blade tensed and spun, pulling a knife from somewhere as he did. As soon as he saw who it was, he relaxed.

"You find him?"

"Yeah, found him, but he won't fucking come with us. Says he's done with switching hells."

Knowing they were talking about Dr. Maestro, I pushed around from behind Blade, ignoring his grumbling. "Take me to him, let me explain who you are. He'll come with me."

The man raised an eyebrow at Blade and spoke over my head to him. "It'll be the only way, unless we knock his ass out and carry him."

I gasped. "Please, he's been hurt enough. Elita had her men do horrible things to him, but he'll trust me. If I tell him y'all are safe to go with, he will. At least let me try? Before you knock him out and hurt him even more."

"Fine, but we need to make it fast. The others are here and shit's gonna hit the fan any second."

Blade kept me between him and the other men as we jogged through the dark house to another wing. Each of the men pulled out handguns as we moved along the hallway and handled them with the confidence of men who knew how to use them. Which they proved when we came to a well-lit hallway containing three guards with semi-automatic weapons.

Blade shoved me down and fired at the same time as the other two men. The three guards dropped, dead before they even saw us. With a firm grip under my arms, Blade lifted me back to my feet and we continued down the hallway. This whole thing was so far outside what I'd ever experienced, I had no way to process it.

Before I could get too caught up in the easy way these men had killed my uncle's guards, I found myself being moved past another biker and into a room where Dr.

Maestro was standing in the furthest corner. Trembling, he was pressing back against the walls as though they'd open up and swallow him.

"Hey, Dr. Maestro." He was frozen like a scared deer, so I made myself as cheery as possible, under the circumstances. I really wished he'd given me his first name at some point. Seemed ridiculous after all we'd been through that I was still calling him something so formal. "I need you to come with me now. Remember? I told you Blade would come for us, that he'd already been coming to rescue you? Well, this is him, and his club. We're safe with them, I promise."

I held out my hand to him as I moved closer, while the noises in the house grew in intensity and volume. Gunfire, shouts and pounding footsteps. I ignored it all, knowing the four men standing behind me had us covered.

"We really need to get moving before my uncle comes looking for us. He's gonna be really mad that I'm not where he left me. He knows I'm protective of you, so he'll come here next, looking for me. He knows I wouldn't leave you behind."

The look in his gaze broke my heart. Elita had seriously fucked with his head, along with his body. I had no clue what his life would be like once we got to freedom, but I vowed to help him any way I could. I wriggled my fingers, desperate for him to take my hand so we could get out of here. Slowly, he reached for me and wrapped his long fingers around my wrist. I copied his grip and gently pulled him from his hiding spot.

"C'mon, let's get out of here."

We got to the door and one of the men had his phone to his ear and held his palm up for us to stay put. After saying a few words I didn't catch, he pocketed the phone.

"The rear of the house is a no go. Looks like we're gonna have to head out the front somehow."

Bank, according to the name tag on his vest, spoke up. "Wouldn't it be better to find another room to wait it out in? If we walk out there while bullets are still flying, I don't like our chances of getting everyone out alive."

Blade nodded. "Yeah, as Veronica said, this room is the logical place that Jovan will come looking for her, but if we move to another room, we should be safe enough."

Remembering Blade's words about them burning this place down had me leading them to my uncle's office. Once we were inside, I removed myself from Dr. Maestro's grip and went for the painting on the wall behind his desk. It was so fucking clichéd but I didn't care about that right now. I tore the frame from the wall and spun the dial on the revealed safe. Putting in the code

I'd seen him enter so many years ago, I prayed he hadn't changed it. A click had me releasing the breath I was holding as I swung the heavy door open.

"Veronica, what are you doing?"

"You said to take anything that matters. He has my mother's jewelry in here, my father's wedding ring." *At least I hope he has it in there.*

Pulling out boxes of papers, I tossed them on the desk, not caring about his blackmail material at all. I was vaguely aware of some of the other men, the ones that weren't wearing Charon MC vests were gathering up what I was tossing, but I didn't give a fuck. Finally, I found the box. A lacquered black jewelry box that had so proudly sat on my mother's dresser my whole life. Gripping it carefully with both hands, I lifted it free of the safe and moved to sit on the couch before I opened the lid. Nestled against the royal blue satin were my parents' wedding rings, along with several of Mom's necklaces and bracelets. I ran a finger over them, tears stinging my eyes.

"I didn't think I've ever see these again."

He'd threatened to sell them so many times—each and every time I tried to stand up to him. It appeared he'd sold at least some of them as there were pieces missing that I knew should be here. I swiped at the tears. He hadn't sold them because he needed the money, but more likely to teach me a lesson. I doubted he went to much effort so I'd go see the local pawn shops, maybe ask Keys to see if he could track them down. Although, really, it was something so unimportant in the big scheme of things.

"Little dove, don't cry. You're breaking my heart."

"He's sold some of it. The diamond necklace my father bought my mother for their tenth wedding anniversary isn't here."

He crouched down in front of me and I looked from the contents of the box, up into his brilliant blue eyes.

"We'll search the local pawn dealers for it, and if we can't find it anywhere, we'll get another one made. It's a thing, sweetheart, replaceable. You are not. For now, I need you to focus on getting out of here, okay? We'll worry about the necklace and anything else missing later, yeah?"

I nodded. He was right, of course. All material things were replaceable. He leaned in and after frowning at my busted lip, pressed a kiss to my temple before standing and moving back toward the door and the other men. The one who'd been on his phone earlier lifted it to his ear again, then frowned before hanging up, all without speaking a word. I was pretty sure that didn't bode well.

Chapter 11

Blade

Tank, one of the Cowboys who'd come in with the other van, put his phone away but didn't look happy. "They need us out there. We've got the place surrounded, and taken out the exterior guards, but Jovan's got his men covering all the exits from the inside with semis. Our men can't get near enough to take the fuckers out. It's going to be up to us to clear them an entrance."

I closed my eyes for a moment. Fuck it all. How many men did this bastard have at his disposal? I turned and looked over at Veronica. She was still sitting on the couch with her mother's jewelry box open on her lap, but was looking at us as though she'd heard what Tank had said. The doctor had shifted to stand behind the couch, behind Veronica. He was a shell of the arrogant prick who I'd met in the ER last month. I had to wonder what Elita had done to the poor bastard to do so much damage in such a short period of time.

Veronica cleared her throat as she closed the lid on the box. "We'll stay here while you go do your thing. We'll be fine."

I huffed out a breath. I didn't like it, but it was the safest option we had open to us. We needed to go out there and kill her uncle's men. That would be harder if we had those two with us. The doctor was a PTSD mess waiting to happen, and Veronica was too fucking sweet and had already been through too much. Not to mention the whole no shoes thing they both had going on. Neither of them needed to see us go on a killing spree.

"Fine, but you two don't move from this fucking room, you hear me? And you lock that door behind us."

They both nodded before Veronica stood and moved over to the door, ready to flip the lock. I gave her a fast kiss, inwardly cursing when she winced before lifting her fingers to cover her split lip. Forcing myself to focus back on the situation, I pressed a knife into her hand that wasn't covering her face before I slipped out into the hallway.

"So, how many knives you got on you exactly?"

I raised a brow at Riff, the other Cowboy with us. "Enough. They don't call me Blade for nothing. And I prefer knives, they're quieter."

"Guns are quicker, simpler."

"Only if you don't know what you're doing."

With a wink, I shrugged a shoulder. I was as fast throwing a knife as I was pulling a trigger. And collecting a knife from a body was much simpler than collecting bullets and casings. But I let it go, we didn't have time to debate weapon choice right at the moment.

Tank chuckled before growing serious. "Right, I think it'll be easier to clear a way through the side entrance. From reports, Jovan's got most of his men out the front and back."

Once we all nodded our agreement, we all headed after Tank toward the side entrance. Allowing my inner beast to rise up again, I left my gun holstered and pulled a knife into each hand, ready to either throw or slice. The house was still fairly dark. At a guess, they were trying to make it harder for our guys to see in. Unfortunately for them, they still didn't realize we were already inside. Apparently no one had yet missed the three guards we'd already dispatched.

The closer we got, the slower and more careful we had to approach, to not draw their attention. Tank signaled for me to take the lead, pointing to my weapons as I slipped past him. I gave him a nod that I understood. Take out who I could silently, then they'd shoot the rest. Three men stood with their weapons pointed outside, but none of them were watching their backs. We might be able to do this silently. With a few hand signals, I had Tank and Bank by my side with knives in their fists. Riff stood back and had his gun up and aimed at the men facing away from us.

Adrenaline pumped through my veins, heightening my senses as I crept up behind my target. My beast was roaring in my ears, ready for blood. Keeping the other two men in my peripheral vision, I made sure we struck at the same time, grabbing fistfuls of hair and swiping our blades across their throats in one smooth, fast movement. Snagging their guns, we lowered them together with the bodies to the ground before we did a final check for more of Jovan's men. When we saw none, I flicked open the lock on the door and shoved it open while Tank used his phone to pass the information on to the men outside that they could now enter.

In order to not clue in Jovan's guards on the other doors that we'd breeched the building, only the men closest to this entry point came in after us. We were now a dozen men strong and I was torn over what to do. I wanted to be the one to put an end to Allen Jovan's life, but I also wanted to get back to Veronica's side to make sure she was safe. The men who flowed through the door spread out, heading to the other entrances to take out more of Jovan's men.

"Anyone seen the fucker himself?"

Tank shook his head. "No one's reported in with a visual."

"You think he escaped before we got here?"

Riff grunted. "No way. If his niece is here, so is he. No way a man puts all that time, money and effort into retrieving her, just to abandon her. He's here."

Riff was right. There's no way Allen would leave Veronica behind. "Let's go back to the office and grab her and the doctor, get them out of here. Then we can go hunting. He's been breathing for way too long."

With a sudden sense of urgency, I jogged back down the hallway. I skidded to a stop when I came around the corner and saw the door wasn't closed all the way. What the fuck? Was Veronica trying to see if the way was clear?

Veronica's voice filled the air, "Don't touch me!"

Oh, hell no.

I turned back to Tank. "Found the fucker, and he's mine."

Bank and Riff were also beside me but like Tank, they didn't say a word as I rolled my neck, allowed the beast free rein, and strode forward. As I struck the door with my foot, flinging it open, I had my arm raised, ready to throw. My blade left my fingers as I stepped into the room. He let loose a curse when the metal sank deep into his shoulder. Predicting he'd spin just as he had, I'd aimed for his upper torso, not wanting to risk hurting Veronica if I went for his neck and missed. That, and I didn't want his end to be fast. Fucker deserved to suffer first.

"Get away from my woman."

At my growled words, he lifted his other arm to reveal a gun with a silencer on it. Time slowed down, the seconds dragging out. I lifted my other blade to throw, but knew it wouldn't be fast enough to save myself. I heard guns behind me being cocked but, in the end, it wasn't one of the men who saved my life, it was my woman. Curses filled the air as bullets flew and Veronica lunged at her uncle and drove into his side hard, taking them both down. I rushed forward to get her away from him, praying none of the bullets had hit her. Jovan had dropped his weapon and had his fingers wrapped around Veronica's biceps, holding her to him. His eyes were on hers and looked both pained and shocked.

"Why, baby? You're mine, I always looked after you. I came and rescued you!"

Her voice was rough, sounding like she had a sore throat, when she replied. "You're a monster. I was your niece! And you ruined me. You took away everything I ever cared about. You fucking killed my parents. You *never* looked after me, only ever yourself."

His knuckles turned white as his grip tightened on her. I attacked one hand, gripping his pinky and wrenching it back until he released his hold on her. Tank was on the other side, doing the same thing on his other hand. Once he released his grasp, we both slammed his wrists back against the floor and Bank wrapped an arm around Veronica.

"C'mon, honey. It's over."

I ran my eyes over her, looking for wounds, but all I could see was blood. Was it hers? Or his? I looked back at her uncle and had to smile at the knife embedded in his stomach. Veronica had stabbed him with the blade I'd given her. That was my girl.

"You'll always be mine, Victoria. No one will ever have you like I have. You'll never wear another's mark like you do mine—"

Her scream cut off his words and she broke free of Bank's hold. She stepped up to her uncle and delivered a hard kick between his legs, making the fucker howl and the rest of us wince. No doubt the bastard deserved it, but no man could watch another's balls copping that kind of abuse and not flinch at least a little.

"I was never yours. *Never.*"

She dropped to her knees and started pawing at my belt. It took me a second to realize what she was wanting. My heart broke a little more for her. She was trying to get my larger knife.

"Tank, take this."

I transferred Jovan's wrist I held to Tank, who shifted to hold both of the dying man's wrists tightly against the floor. I took my knife out and moved until I was behind Veronica. I put the hilt of the weapon in her palm, wrapping my hand around hers.

"Let me help you."

It was actually not that easy to stab into the heart if you didn't know what you were doing. She'd most likely hit a rib and not get very far at all. As much as I wanted to be the one to end her enemy for her, I couldn't deny her this. But I intended to help her, guide her so it was over as quickly as possible for her.

I looked up into the frightened gaze of Allen Jovan. "If we had more time, I'd tie you down to die slowly from that gut wound. But we don't have that kinda time, so you get the fast end you don't deserve."

Veronica moved our hands, getting ready to drop the blade. I shifted it, whispering in her ear when she tried to fight my control over the weapon. "Need to go between the ribs, little dove."

With a small nod, she allowed me to shift the aim. She pushed a little, but hesitated when blood welled around the tip of the sharp knife. She shook her head, her muscles tensing. I was about to pull her away when he spoke up.

"You can't do it. Because you know you're mine, you can't kill your master."

With a growl, she pushed her weight forward against the hilt, as I put some muscle behind it too, making sure the blade sank deep enough to pierce the heart. With wide eyes he gasped before going limp. Tank released him and stood, while I shifted Veronica so she was against my chest, then stood and went to the couch to sit with her. Her body shook and her tears wet my neck but she was silent.

"It's over, little dove. You did it. Saved yourself."

"Ah, fuck."

I turned to see what had Bank cursing. The doctor lay on the carpet, his chest covered in blood. Bank was kneeling at his side, fingers to his throat.

"Oh, no. No!"

Veronica fled from my lap and ran over to them, tearing at the shirt to locate the wound just as Scout and Viper came striding into the room. One look and Scout lifted his phone, punching a button before putting it to his ear.

"Need you in Allen's office, man down with a chest wound."

Then he hung up and took in the rest of the room. "What a fucking mess."

Viper nodded from where he stood beside him. "Tank, Riff, get me everything out of that safe and yank the hard drive out of his computer. I want everything this fucker had of worth before we torch this place."

I caught Veronica's body tense as she worked on the doctor and looked over to see her glance toward the couch. I moved over to grab the jewelry box.

"Don't worry, Veronica, your parents' jewelry is all yours. No one's gonna try to take that from you."

Viper turned toward Veronica, his stern face softening some. "I'm only interested in information, honey. Everything else is all yours."

I thought I saw tears well but she looked back down to her patient before I could be certain.

What a fucking night.

Veronica

After Donna and Keys had loaded up Dr. Maestro and sped off to hospital in the club's ambulance, Blade carried me out through the front of the house to a van Bank had just rolled up in. Blade sat with me, but after a few minutes his tension was driving me nuts.

"I'll be fine. Go help so we can get out of here."

He took my face between his palms and stared directly into my eyes. "Are you sure you're okay? He didn't hurt you before I got to you?"

I lifted my own blood-stained hand to stroke down his face, scraping my nails through his short beard.

"You arrived in time, stop worrying. And I'm more than okay. It's over. My uncle is gone and can't ever hurt me again. Blade, I'm free. Truly free."

He smiled gently before leaning in and brushing kiss after kiss over my mouth, being gentle against the healing split.

"Fuck, I love you, Veronica. So much. Lock the doors and if anyone not wearing a cut comes up to you, get the gun from the glove compartment and shoot them. Okay?"

I gave him a nod. "Got it."

After hitting the locks, I watched him stride back into the house that had been my hell for so long. Leaning my head against the headrest, I watched as various men came in and out, carrying bodies inside or boxes out. They hadn't been kidding about wanting everything from my uncle's office. I hoped they didn't intend to continue my uncle's blackmail tactics but honestly, I didn't have enough energy to worry about that right now.

Guilt over Dr. Maestro was riding me hard. He hadn't looked good when they'd whisked him away. He'd been standing by the window, trying to see what was going on out there when my uncle had come in. He'd barely turned toward the door when he'd been shot. My uncle gave no warning. There was no reason to shoot the doctor, he wasn't a threat at all. Then Blade came storming in, and with everything that happened I'd forgotten about him until Bank found him. How could I have forgotten he was there and injured? I was such a shitty nurse. I prayed he survived. That he had a chance to live a decent life after what he'd been put through due to no fault of his own these past weeks.

A flood of men leaving the house had me sitting up straighter. They all headed to bikes that were parked around the driveway, except for Blade and Bank, who were coming toward me. I flipped the locks and opened the door, slipping onto the ground as Blade got to me. A hint of smoke hit my nose and I looked from him to the house, seeing the red glow in a few of the windows.

"C'mon, sweetheart. Time to get out of here before the authorities get called in about the fire."

I nodded but couldn't look away from the sight of everything my uncle had coveted going up in flames. I didn't fight Blade when he lifted me and got into the van, settling me on his lap. I kept my face toward the fire, still unable to look away. Blade's hand stroked over my head, his fingers combing through my messy curls.

"Love the curls, darlin'."

He buried his face in against them and my heart lightened at the reminder of him wanting to see my hair in its natural state. I liked that Blade loved them, because I loved my curls too, and had missed letting them do their thing over the years.

A smile crept over my face as it sunk in that my uncle was really gone—dead, and soon to be little more than ash. He couldn't control my life anymore, unless I allowed him to. And I refused to give him that much power, especially now he was gone.

"So, Veronica, you gonna go back to being Victoria now?"

I looked away from my uncle's home, closing the door in my mind on everything he'd ever said or done to me, and faced Bank.

"Victoria died a long time ago. I'm Veronica now."

Bank smiled with a nod as he kept driving. Blade guided my head to rest on his chest and I shifted until I had the leather shoved aside so my ear was against the thin shirt over his warm skin. I tucked my hand underneath the material, resting my palm over his left pectoral, his heartbeat soothing me like it always had, and I let my mind empty as the van took me away from my past and into my future.

I woke when Blade shifted out of the vehicle with me still in his arms. With a yawn, I wrapped one arm around his neck while I rubbed my eyes with the other hand before I looked around to see where we were.

"We're at the Satan's Cowboys' clubhouse. We'll stay here till morning then head back to Bridgewater."

"Okay."

I thought about telling him I could walk, but honestly, it felt too good in his arms to want to end it just yet. And considering I still didn't have any shoes, I was sure he'd refuse to put me down anyway. My mother's jewelry box was resting against my tummy, and I picked it up so it wouldn't fall.

"Blade!"

He stopped and I turned to see Mac coming toward us with a bag. "Donna brought a bag of stuff for Veronica." He held it open so I could set the box in, before he closed it and handed it over to me.

"Thank you."

The club was something else. Everyone was so nice. "Head up to the room you had before, get cleaned up. Again. And try to catch some sleep. We'll head home as soon as everyone's awake in the morning."

"Thanks, brother. For everything."

Mac reached out and gripped Blade's shoulder. They stared into each other's eyes, sharing some deep moment I didn't fully comprehend.

"Welcome to club life, Blade. We take care of our own here. Always." He released his hold and turned to face me. "I'm glad we got to you in time, Veronica. You'll be safe here. No one you don't want to see will get anywhere near you, okay?"

I nodded, unsure what to say. Before it got any more awkward, Blade shifted his grip on me and strode off toward a staircase and took me up to a small but clean room.

"This place used to be a hotel. It's a good set-up. You hungry at all, or do you just want a shower and lie down?"

Once the door was shut, he lowered my feet to the floor. I placed the bag on the top of the chest of drawers before I turned back to Blade. He watched me warily, like he was waiting for me to fall apart.

"You came for me. Set me free."

He winced and looked away from me. "It was my fault you got taken in the first place. Your uncle wouldn't have found you if Elita's man hadn't grabbed you."

Now we were here in this room, locked away from the rest of the world, I was feeling giddy with my freedom. My uncle was dead. I wasn't going to allow Blade to tear that away from either of us. I stepped up to him, sliding my palms up his chest, under his cut to push it from his shoulders. He shrugged out of it and tossed the leather on the chair by the door.

"You listening to me, Veronica? All this—" he circled a finger between us, "is because of me. Elita found out what you mean to me and used you to inflict pain on me."

I nodded then leaned in to kiss his lips lightly. "Yep. Then my uncle saw the news report of me being kidnapped and came after me."

His arms wrapped around me. They felt like steel bands holding me to him, as though he were scared if he released me, I'd fly away. Silly man. Now I was finally free to live my life, the last thing I wanted was to leave the best thing that had happened to me in years.

"How can you even look at me?"

His deep voice was rough and filled with pain. He honestly was taking on all the guilt over what had happened.

"I like looking at you. You really are quite pretty."

He growled and shook his head before staring into my gaze. "Stop joking, Veronica. This is fucking serious—"

I pressed two fingers over his mouth.

"I know it is, Blade. Trust me, I fully understand how serious this whole fucked-up mess has been. You didn't hand me over to Elita, nor did you call in my uncle. That's on them, not you. It was their choice to come after me. You're no more to blame than I am. If I hadn't hidden away in Bridgewater, none of this would have happened either. Is it therefore my fault that I brought my uncle into your world? Handed Elita a way to hurt you?"

"That's just plain stupid. It was never your fault that a fucking lunatic pedophile came after you and forced you to go into hiding."

I shifted to cup his cheeks in my palms, ignoring the blood and dirt that stained them. "Nor was it yours. Please, don't let misplaced guilt steal our future from us. I'm free, Blade. For the first time in my life, I'm free to live however I want."

"Darlin', that's kinda what has me scared right now. You can go anywhere, do anything… why the fuck would you want to stay in small town Texas with a scarred-up ex-mobster-turned-biker like me?"

I smiled at him. His showing me his vulnerable side was even more endearing than him storming into my uncle's stronghold like a warrior of old to rescue me.

"I like Bridgewater. I have friends there, my home. Memories of a man who showed me what it was to love." I ran a palm down his arm, over the button up shirt he wore that covered his nearly healed burns. "Blade, my beautifully broken prince, we all have scars. Some are visible to the eye, some not. But we all have them." I went for his buttons, undoing them as quickly as I could. "Scars mean we survived. They show the world how strong we are. Trust me, Blade, I have no issue at all with any of your scars, other than the fact it hurts me that you were injured that severely in the first place. And the whole ex-mobster-now-biker thing? That just means my man is a badass who has the connections to save my hide from any shit that might find me. Again, not something I have an issue with. My uncle might be gone, but who knows what the future will bring?"

With an impatient growl, he ripped his shirt off, popping the final buttons across the room, before he reached for my hips and pulled me flush against him. "Doesn't matter what it brings, little dove. No one will ever get near enough to hurt you again." He lifted a hand to bury it in my curls, using his grip to tilt my face up to his. "You're mine. I honestly never thought I'd have a woman of my own. That dream died when I was sixteen. But here you are. I tried to resist you, to not fall, but I couldn't help it. You're just too fucking perfect." He paused and his gaze switched between my eyes and my mouth twice before he lowered his mouth to mine, kissing me with so much emotion, my heart skipped a beat. Even the sting from the cut to my lower lip didn't take away from the moment. I rested my palms on his ribs, letting his heat soak into me as I leaned into his embrace.

He lifted away from me for a moment.

"Fuck, Veronica. You understand that you're it for me, don't you? I love you and can't fucking breathe without you. Say you'll stay with me, be mine always."

He kissed me again before I could get a word out. By the time he let me up for air again I was panting and could barely remember my own name, let alone his question.

"You gonna answer me, my little dove?"

"Ah, what was the question again?"

My voice was husky with my arousal and I wriggled against his body, enjoying the feel of his hard muscles against me, even with the barrier of clothes. His laugh was dark and sent tingles down my spine. He wrapped his hands around my hips and lifted me. My legs wrapped around his waist automatically and he moved toward a door that I guessed would be a bathroom.

"I asked if you'd be mine for always. Be my old lady? Wear my property patch?"

I thought back to the party I'd been to at the Charon clubhouse. The women I'd met who'd been wearing cuts that had declared them as property of their men.

"I'm still not sure about the whole 'old lady' and 'property' thing."

Now in the bathroom, he set me back on my feet and started to undress me.

"You said you were fine with a biker and that brings with it some fun stuff like new labels. Like I said earlier, a biker's old lady is his one and only. A woman so precious and important to him that he wants to declare it to club and the world. You saw what the other old ladies were wearing at the party, yeah?"

I nodded, "Their *cuts,* but the women had property of written on the back, not Charon MC. I'll never be someone's property, not ever again."

For the most part my uncle had treated me as though I were a prized possession, not a person.

Blade cut his hand through the air, as though he could physically stop my thoughts from going where they were. "It's not like that with the club. You've seen how the Charon women are, at the party, at the bar. How Donna behaves at work. The women in the club are never treated like objects. It's just a label, gorgeous." He chuckled. "Actually, I imagine the old ladies would put their men on their asses pretty damn quickly if they even attempted to treat them that way. It's a respect thing."

He kneeled before me to help remove my pants and shoes, and looking down at him, my heart skipped a beat again. I really wasn't sure about being called an old lady at thirty two, or being labeled property after all my uncle had put me through, but Blade had never treated me with anything other than respect. And he was right, I'd witnessed how the club men treated their women at the bar over the years, and at the club party the other week.

I'd never seen any of the women be mistreated or disrespected.

Even now, when I knew he was on edge and still riding high from my rescue, he was carefully, gently stripping me, before standing remove the rest of his own clothes. I turned and flipped on the shower, letting the water warm as I watched my man stripping down to his delicious skin. Every dip and rise of muscle was beautiful and made my fingers itch to touch them all.

Without another word, he prowled toward me while I backed under the warm spray. His gaze roamed my body along with his hands, heating me up as he cleaned away the day's traumas. He took extra time on my wrists, the grazes from Elita's cuffs only just beginning to heal. The water was tinged red as it ran over us, rinsing all the blood and guilt down the drain and away from us forever. By the time he flipped the tap off, we were both panting. My body was alive and humming, needing more of Blade.

Blade

Veronica was naked and as she dried herself from our shower, she kept a come-fuck-me gaze on me. I wasn't strong enough to resist that much temptation. Not that I was planning on even attempting to. We'd washed away all the shit from our pasts in that shower, and now the future lay open and clean, waiting for us to write the rest of our story. Tossing my own towel aside, I stepped over and wrapped my arms around her, lifting her against me. Her slick pussy rubbed over the underside of my cock and had me groaning as I carried her out of the bathroom. Two steps through the door and I was already too far gone to wait any longer. With my palms cupping her ass, I lifted her up until my cock was lined up with her slick heat. I took one of her tight little nipples in my mouth and sucked on it as I lowered her down over my length. Her fingers dug into my shoulders and the sparks of pain had my cock twitching within her heat.

"Fuck, ba— love."

Dammit, I'd nearly slipped up and called her baby. I didn't want anything to ruin this moment, and throwing her back into her past would be a sure mood killer. Before she could say anything or think about what I nearly said, I pulled her all the way down my length. That had her face level with mine so I could cover her lips with my own, kissing her deeply for a few moments before I tore my mouth from hers and spun us around, pressing her back against the wall so I could get the leverage I needed to fuck her as hard as my body and mind were demanding I take her.

She dug her heels into my ass as she groaned, her channel rippling around my cock as I pounded into her. The events of the evening had me riding the edge. The fact my inner beast hadn't been the one to end her tormentor had me still needing to prove to her that I was man enough to protect her. It was fucked up and stupid, but there it was. My inner caveman needed to fuck her hard to prove I could, to prove she was really here with me and all mine.

The fact she hadn't agreed to be mine forever earlier didn't help.

I buried my face in against her throat, nipping and sucking at the tender skin there as I gripped her hips and tilted them so that with each thrust I ground against her clit. I needed to feel her come apart for me. Her body tensed as her breaths grew shorter.

"Blaaadddde!"

She dragged out my name and I knew she was close. I thrust in deep and circled my hips at the same time as I reached up and twisted one of her nipples. With a gasp, she clenched down and came, drenching my cock with her liquid heat.

"That's it, my little dove, fly for me."

She trembled as she came down and sliding free from her body, I scooped her up and moved to lay her down on the bed. With her eyes closed, she arched her back, stretching her arms up over her head as she rubbed her thighs together and moaned. My girl was still hungry, which suited me just fine because I was fucking starving. I was also close to coming myself so needed to take a few minutes to let my cock settle down.

Pressing a knee to the bed, I grabbed her ankles and guided them wide. Loose-limbed from her climax, she didn't fight me positioning her legs how I wanted them, which was spread wide so I could see her smooth, glistening center that was coated in her sweet honey. That was all fucking mine. Lowering myself down onto the bed, I slipped my palms under her ass to hold her up so I could really make a meal out of her.

My first lick left her squealing and me groaning. She tasted so fucking good. I went back for more and within moments, she had a hand tangled in my hair, gripping me to her. *Like I'd be going anywhere any time soon.* I alternated between fucking her with my tongue and sucking on her lips and clit. When she started to push her hips up against my face, I shifted my grip. Flicking her clit with my tongue, I gently bit down as I thrust two fingers inside her core, rubbing over her g-spot as I continued to torment her little pearl with my mouth. Her sobs were music to my ears as her body began to tremble beneath me. Adding a third finger, I roughly shoved them deep as I nipped her clit again and she blew apart for me once more.

My cock throbbed for its turn and I very nearly came all over the fucking sheets as I took a few extra moments to lap at the cream she'd gifted me. The moment I looked up at her writhing, flushed body, I couldn't hold back from claiming her any longer. I knew I should wrap up but I couldn't bring myself to do it. It wouldn't be the first time I'd gone bare with her. I needed to feel her around me, skin to skin. Needed to fill her up, empty my seed inside her and know it was there, marking her as mine. If she got pregnant, it was just another connection between us. Something else to tie us together for the rest of our lives.

Moving up, I kneeled between her thighs and with a firm grip on her sweat-slicked hips, I shifted her forward over my thighs so the head of my cock was lined up with her opening. She was tight after her orgasms and the feel of her body yielding to me as I thrust balls deep on one slide had my eyes rolling back while she cried out my name again.

Sweetest fucking sound I'd ever heard.

With slow, deep thrusts, I kept her on edge, watching how her body moved with each of my movements inside her. Her tits caught my attention and my mouth watered at the way they bounced in time with my thrusts. In a single, smooth movement, I leaned forward, punching a fist into the mattress near her shoulder to support my weight as I lowered my mouth to take a nipple between my teeth. I gave it a tug as I sped up my thrusts, pounding into her roughly. Just how I knew she liked it. One of her hands was buried in the sheets while she lifted the other one to wrap around my head. I fucking loved how she held me to her, like she never wanted me to leave. I knew for certain that I'd never want to let her go.

Wrapping my free hand around her other breast, I tweaked, twisted and tugged on her nipple as I continued to torment the one in my mouth. She writhed beneath me, begged, pleaded and cried out until my own arousal reached a point of no return. Sparks flew down my spine and landed in my balls, drawing them up, ready to shoot. Releasing her tits, I sat up on my knees and with a firm grip on her hips once more, I pounded into my woman, releasing every ounce of my passion for her, my love and possession, all the worry I'd felt while she'd been away from me. All of it, I poured out into every slide of my cock into her body. When my orgasm was moments away and my cock began to kick within her, I shifted my thumb to press against her clit, hoping she was far enough gone that she wouldn't slip back into her past at my movement.

Her body stiffened, but thankfully not out of fear. It was arousal that had her stiffening, arching her back then screaming out as she came for me a third time. Her walls rippling around my cock had me coming harder and for longer than I ever had before, filling her up with all the seed I had to give.

Once the storm passed, I dropped down over her and rolled us to the side so I wouldn't crush her. Keeping her gathered in close to me, I pressed a kiss to her temple and tried to catch my breath. She snuggled in closer, resting her ear over my heart. I had no clue why she found listening to my heartbeat so enthralling, but I fucking loved it. She murmured something but I couldn't hear her, so with a finger under her chin, I tilted her face up.

"What was that, gorgeous?"

"I said, yes, I'll be your old lady."

I stopped breathing for a moment. Did she just say what I thought she said?

"Say it again."

"I love you, Jared Walker. I'm all yours."

I tightened my hold on her for a second or two before I released her and rolled her over onto her back, covering her with my body and began peppering her face with kisses. She giggled and wrapped her arms around my neck as I nibbled up her jaw.

"Luckiest man in the world right now. Got the best old lady out there."

She winced and I laughed. "What? Don't like the title you just claimed?"

"It's gonna take some getting used to. Not sure I'll ever like being called old, Blade."

I kissed her again, giving her nose a little nip after I pulled away from her mouth. "You'll get used it to soon enough once you start hanging around the club more." She was a wet fucking dream lying below me, grinning and flushed with her arousal. "If I could, I'd take you again right now but I still need another couple of minutes to recover from the last round."

My cock was twitching but it wasn't quite up to the task just yet, and I suspected after how rough I'd been with her, she'd be sore too.

"Yeah, let's give it a few hours recovery time before we go having sex again."

I nuzzled in against her neck, using my beard to tickle her tender skin. "You sore, love? Was I too rough?"

I didn't think I'd been, but wanted to make sure.

"You were perfect, but, yeah, I'm feeling a little sore." A yawn cut off her words. "And tired. I haven't really slept in days."

I knew I should be a gentleman and go get a cloth to clean her up, but fuck it all, I liked the idea of her falling to sleep while she still wore me inside and out. So, instead of leaving the bed for the bathroom, I leaned down to grab the sheets we'd shoved out of the way earlier and covered her up.

"Get some sleep, gorgeous. We'll clean up in the morning."

"Uh huh."

With that sleepy reply, she nuzzled her way back in against my chest, her palm over my heart and was breathing deeply within moments. I took a little longer to doze off because I was enjoying having my woman safe in my arms too much to want to miss out on a second of it. But eventually, the day caught up with me and I followed her into sleep, feeling like the luckiest bastard on earth.

Epilogue

Veronica

It was a week after our rescue and Dr. Eric Maestro – I'd finally learned his first name – was still in the hospital. As soon as he'd been stable enough to move, we'd brought him here to Bridgewater where we could make sure he received the care and support he needed. He was physically recovering well from the gunshot wound, which had thankfully missed his heart and lungs, but I was still worried about his mental health. Elita had really screwed him up.

I was walking out of his room, having stopped to visit him after finishing my shift, when my phone rang. Seeing it was Silk, I answered with a smile.

"Hey, girl. What's up?"

"Got some free time tonight if you wanna come in? We can get started on your piece."

I'd spoken with her earlier in the week about doing a cover-up over my uncle's tattoo. Silk's enthusiasm had both excited and scared the crap out of me. I still wondered if she was going to try to talk me into some huge thing that would cover half my torso.

"Just let me check with Blade, but I should be good to come over. What time?"

"Go get yourself some dinner with your man then head over to the shop. I'll see you later!"

I hung up and with a spring in my step, headed out the doors and glanced around the parking lot for Blade. When I didn't see him, I frowned. Where was he? Every day this week he'd been here to give me a ride after work, either home or to the clubhouse.

"Hey, Veronica, need a lift?"

I turned to face Donna, who'd just finished up too. "Looks like it. Have you heard about anything going on with the club?"

She pulled her phone out to check it and shook her head. "Nope, no news. I guess they just got busy talking or something. Let's go see what they're up to."

I followed her to her car and slid into the passenger seat.

"I'm going to see Silk later."

"Oh, so you're going ahead with the cover up, then?"

I'd spent a lot of time with Donna this week, chatting about everything.

"I think so. It's the last reminder of him. I want it gone."

"I can understand that."

For the rest of the drive I let my mind wander on what Silk had drawn up for me. Before I knew it, we were pulling up in the lot outside the clubhouse. It was late afternoon on a Friday, so things were just starting to get busy as the various brothers and their old ladies got off from work and headed in for a night of fun, drinks and laughter. As we got out, Donna paused, frowning at one of the cars in the lot.

"What's up?"

"I don't know that car and the plates are out of state."

I looked more closely and saw that she was right. They were Arizona plates.

"Anyone from the club moved up there recently?"

She shook her head as she strode across the lot for the door. The prospect manning the door tucked his phone away and opened the door for us and I gave him a smile of thanks as we passed inside. Mac came barreling down the hallway in such a way that I figured the prospect must have just called him. My blood turned to ice in my veins.

"What happened?"

"It's okay, Veronica. Nothing bad's happened."

I frowned at him. "Well, where the hell is Blade then?"

"He's busy at the moment, but I need you to come see Scout for a second before we go find him. Okay?"

Donna patted my arm. "Come find me once you're done, 'kay?"

"Sure."

I absently gave her a nod before I followed Mac down the hallway to an office. He paused at the doorway.

"Brace yourself."

Every word the man uttered made me more anxious. "Can we just get this over with already?"

With a chuckle he swung the door in. I gasped at who was revealed. Mr. Conway, the lawyer who'd helped me escape all those years ago sat at the desk, facing Scout.

"Mr. Conway? Is that really you? What on earth are you doing here?"

I rushed over to him while he stood, and wrapped my arms around the older man. I could never repay what this gentleman had done for me all those years ago. His hand patted my back.

"When I heard and saw what happened at your uncle's place so soon after hearing about your kidnapping, I knew it had to involve you somehow. I've always kept tabs on where you were since you first left, so I knew you'd be back here in Bridgewater now it's all over."

I shook my head and brushed away the tears that had leaked out. "You came all this way just to see if I was okay?"

Was the Arizona plated car his? Had he moved away to get free from my uncle too, at some point?

"Oh, it's not so far from Greenswood, but no, as much as I'm extremely pleased to see you in such good health, the reason I came was to return some things to you." He turned and lifted a briefcase from the floor, laying it flat on the desk before opening it. Curiosity had me shifting to watch over his shoulder as he pulled the first of several velvet bags out.

"All of these are rightfully yours, my dear."

I took the bag, opening it and tipping it into my palm. A sob caught in my throat when my mother's diamond necklace landed in my hand.

"How?"

The one word was all I could get out past the lump in my throat.

"Your uncle wasn't the only one with contacts, Veronica. And many citizens of Greenswood hated that man. The first time he took a piece from your mother's jewelry collection into the local pawn shop, the owner came to me. He'd known I was friends with your parents and he didn't know what to do with the piece. He didn't want you to lose it because your uncle was a bastard. Allen had explained to him he was selling it as punishment for your disobedience, and had told him there would no doubt be more as you were stubborn. From there, I struck a deal with him that I would cover the cost of anything he'd brought in and make sure it was all kept safe for when you were found and free of him."

I returned the diamond to the bag and he handed me the others, each one revealing another of my mother's treasures.

"I already didn't know how to thank you for all you've done for me, and now this?"

I looked up into his smiling face, trying to blink away the new flood of tears. He reached a hand out to me, and I placed all the bags on Scout's desk so I could fully embrace the man who'd played such a big part in helping me get my life on track.

"My dear girl, seeing you happy and living a life filled with love and friendship is all the thanks I need."

With a sniffle, I pulled back. "Will you stay a while? Meet my man?"

He gave me a pat on my shoulder before he turned to close his briefcase. "I wish I could, but I need to get going. I'm getting a little too old to be driving late at night, I'm afraid. But I did get to meet your man earlier. Nice fellow. You've done well for yourself." When he turned back to me, he held out a business card. "If you ever need anything, don't hesitate to call. Even if it's just to chat a while."

Then he turned and left me there, stunned silent as Scout and Mac shifted to stand in front of me.

"You doing okay?"

"Ah, yeah. I think so. That was so unexpected. How much money must he have spent? I want to pay him back."

Scout nodded. "Before you came in, we spoke about your uncle's estate. Not in depth as he couldn't break client confidentiality. But he made it pretty clear that you are your uncle's only remaining relative so are entitled to his estate. The house was a total loss with the fire, but he had insurance and other assets. I dare say, you'll shortly become rather wealthy, Veronica."

"Oh."

I couldn't process this turn of events. I was so used to bad shit happening, I wasn't sure what to do with this sudden influx of good fortune.

"How about I lock up your mother's jewels in here for now and we go get a drink?"

"Ah, yeah, sure. Um, where's Blade?"

Mac chuckled. "Seems it's the day for surprise visitors. C'mon, I'll go introduce you to Suzette and Aaron. Blade's mom and brother."

I stumbled at Mac's words and caught myself on the door frame. "Are you serious? His mom and brother are here?"

Mac gave me a smirk. "Scout's honor, I'm telling you the truth."

Scout knocked his shoulder against Mac's as he passed him.

"Very funny, brother. C'mon, let's go grab that drink and move out to the backyard. They were heading out there last I heard."

Scout locked his office door then followed Mac and me down to the bar.

"What's your poison?"

"Gin and tonic, thanks."

He relayed the order to the prospect behind the bar and moments later he turned around with two glasses. My clear drink and an amber one. I raised an eyebrow as he handed me both.

"Maker's for your man. Guessing he'll be looking for it by now."

I held Mac's gaze as I took the glasses from him. "You've known Blade a long time, right?"

He nodded. "About twenty years, give or take. Why?"

"Have you met his family before? Know what they're like?"

"Well, until today, I didn't even know the man had a brother, so sorry I can't help you with the history. But they both seemed nice enough when they rolled up earlier today."

He led me through the bar and down the hallway. As we came to the kitchen, Eagle came out with his son Raven in his arms.

"Oh sh— I mean darn. Hey, Eagle, could you call Silk for me? Maybe explain what's going on here and that I won't make it in tonight?"

He gave me a wink at my nearly cussing in front of Raven. "Sure thing, sugar. I'm sure she'll be here once she hears the news."

After a quick thanks, I was back following Mac to the yard. He opened the door and I headed out into the late afternoon sun. Blade jumped up from where he was sitting at the picnic table I'd seen that club whore get fucked on at the last party. *I hope they scrub those things down regularly.* He wrapped an arm around my waist and pressed a kiss to my temple as he took his drink from my hand.

"Hey, little dove. Sorry I couldn't pick you up from work."

I tilted my head up to press a quick kiss to his lips. "That's okay. You've had a busy afternoon, I hear."

His grin was wide and his piercing blue eyes were sparkling with delight and it warmed my heart. After all he'd suffered, he deserved this happiness. We both did.

"I never expected them to drive all the way from Phoenix and turn up here unannounced like this. I called them last weekend. After everything that had happened I wanted to make sure Elita hadn't gone after them, and to let them know the threat over all of us was now gone. Mom was happy with my news, but didn't say a damn thing about visiting."

That explained the car with the out-of-state plates. I loved seeing my man so damn happy and couldn't wait to officially meet his family, who had stood from the table and were waiting for us to get over there already.

"Take me to meet them?"

Blade

With my arm around my woman, I led her over to where my mom and brother were sitting, watching us.

"I heard you had a visitor too."

"Yeah, Mr. Conway came to return the missing jewelry. He was buying it whenever my uncle sold a piece."

I gave her hip a squeeze before I returned my palm to the center of her back. "I met him earlier. Nice man. Thanked him for helping you get away all those years ago. I'm surprised he's not still with you?"

I'd had a chat with him earlier when he'd first arrived. I rather felt like I was meeting her father with the grilling he gave me once he found out we were together. I could totally see that man giving Veronica away at our wedding one day.

She shook her head. "Nah, said he needed to get home before it got too dark. I'm thinking I might head up and visit him every now and then, though. And once my uncle's estate gets settled, I intend to pay him back for everything he spent on me over the years."

That made me chuckle. "I can't see him accepting your money, but we'll work out some way to pay him back, I'm sure. Now, let me introduce you to my mother, Suzette, and my baby brother, Aaron.

"You know, I'm twenty-eight years old, you can quit with the baby brother thing any time now."

I rolled my eyes as he leaned in and gave Veronica a kiss on the cheek. "It's nice to meet you, sis."

She blushed and stammered until my mom moved Aaron out of the way and drew my girl in for a hug.

"Welcome to the family, dear. Jared's told us all about you. It's so wonderful to meet the woman who finally managed to crack through his shell."

My own cheeks heated at my mother's words and I was extremely glad that the other club members had left us alone out here to do our thing. And that Mac had gone back inside after delivering my woman out here to me. I was pretty sure if any of them heard some of the crap my mom was saying, I'd never live it down. Made me grateful I already had a road name, really.

"Jared?"

"Sorry, Mom, what did you say?"

I lifted my glass to take a mouthful as I focused back on the conversation.

"She doesn't have a ring yet, son. What's the hold up?"

I sucked down the liquid into my wind pipe and started coughing. By the time I could talk again, Veronica was in a fit of giggles that would have been adorable if she wasn't laughing at me nearly choking to death.

"Seriously, woman?"

She blinked up at me with falsely innocent eyes.

"Sorry, honey. It just reminded me of that night in Styxx, when I saw you there staring at me and choked on my drink."

Aaron let out a hoot of laughter. "What goes around, comes around, brother. I bet you laughed at her too."

I growled at the pair of them. "I did no such thing, I went and waited outside the bathroom for her to come out to check she was okay."

After I had a chuckle at the fact she'd been so shocked to see me again she'd inhaled her drink. But I wasn't admitting that.

I turned back to my mother, "It'll happen soon, Mom. Can't give away all my secrets though, so you'll just have to wait."

I gave Veronica a wink as she stood there with her mouth agape for a moment before she lifted her drink to cover her shock by taking a mouthful of what I suspected was a strong gin and tonic.

"I better be the first number you dial after you pop the question. We'll make sure we come back down to help celebrate."

Now stuck for words myself, I thunked my glass on the table and pulled my mother in for a hug, holding her to me tightly. I hadn't seen either of them in years. I'd called a few times a year and Mom would text the odd photo of Aaron but I hadn't been able to hug her for way too long. Veronica's hand smoothed up my back and I had to squeeze my eyes shut against the burn of tears.

After all these years, all these struggles, here now, I had everything I'd ever dreamed of. My mom, brother and woman all alive and well, safe from our pasts and able to live our futures to the fullest.

The End

Other Charon MC Books:

Book 1:
Inking Eagle

The sins of her father will be her undoing… unless a hero rides to her rescue.

As the 15th anniversary of the 9/11 attacks nears, Silk struggles to avoid all reminders of the day she was orphaned. She's working hard in her tattoo shop, Silky Ink, and working even harder to keep her eyes and her hands off her bodyguard, Eagle. She'd love to forget her sorrows in his strong arms.

But Eagle is a prospect in the Charon MC, and her uncle is the VP. As a Daughter of the Club, she's off limits to the former Marine. But not for long. As soon as he patches in, he intends to claim Silk for his old lady. He'll wear her ink, and she'll wear his patch.

Too late, they learn that Silk's father had dark secrets, ones that have lived beyond his grave. When demons from the past come for Silk, Eagle will need all the skills he learned in the Marines to get his woman back safe, and keep her that way.

Book 2:
Fighting Mac

She's no sleeping beauty, but then he's no prince - just a biker warrior to the rescue.

For the past three years Claire 'Zara' Flynn has been at the mercy of narcolepsy and cataplexy attacks. But after she witnesses a shooting by the ruthless Iron Hammers MC, her problems get a whole lot worse. She's now a marked woman, on the run for her life.

Former Marine Jacob 'Mac' Miller has a good life with the Charon MC. He works in the club gym and teaches self-defense classes - in the hopes of saving other women from the violent death his sister suffered. When the pretty new waitress at a local cafe catches his attention, he wants her in his bed. But there's a problem. She's clearly scared of all bikers. Wanting to help her, he talks her into coming to his class. Mac soon realizes he wants to keep her close in more ways than one. But can he, when his club's worst enemies come after her?

When Zara disappears, Mac and his brothers must go to war to get her back. Because this time, she wakes up in a terrible place... surrounded by other desperate women, and guarded by the Iron Hammers MC. Can her leather-clad prince ride to the rescue in time to save her from hell?

Book 3:
Chasing Taz

He lived his life one conquest at a time. She calculated her every move… until she met him.

Former Marine Donovan 'Taz' Lee might appear to be a carefree Aussie bloke living it up as a member of the Texan motorcycle club, Charon MC, but the truth is so much more complicated. With blood and tears haunting his past and threatening to destroy his future, Taz is completely unprepared for the woman of his dreams, when she comes in and knocks him on his ass. Literally.

Felicity "Flick" Vaughn joined the FBI to get answers behind her brother's dishonorable discharge and abandonment of his family. Knowing Taz was a part of her brother's final mission, she agrees to partner with him to go after a bigger club, The Satan's Cowboys MC.

However, nothing in life is ever simple and Flick is totally unprepared to have genuine feelings for the sexy

Aussie. When secrets are revealed and their worlds are busted wide open, will they be strong enough to still be standing when the dust settles?

Book 4:
Claiming Tiny

Some rules were meant to be broken.

After being raised in foster care, Ryan 'Tiny' Nelson has no plans to settle down. But that idea goes right out the window when Missy shows up at the clubhouse. One taste of the Charon MC's newest club whore and he's hooked.

Love is the last thing on Mercedes 'Missy' Soto's mind when she runs to the Charon MC for protection. But the first time Tiny wraps his arms around her, he captures her heart in the process.

When things start unravelling, Missy panics and runs. Will Tiny find her in time to give her a Christmas to remember, or will he lose her forever once her past catches up with her?

Book 5:
Saving Scout

Nothing worthwhile in life ever comes fast or easy.

Twenty five years after first meeting the Charon MC's president, Scout, Marie is still waiting for him to realize they're meant to be together. But instead, he comes to her asking she hire his ex. Frustrated with his continued rejection, she leaves town for the weekend to clear her head and maybe find a man who'll help her forget her infatuation.

When Scout first met Marie, she was way too young, and he hadn't been looking to settle down. Over the years, he'd never bothered to rethink his stance. When he learns Marie has fled town, he panics and realizes he needs to step up and claim what has always been his. Tracking her down, he approaches her at her hotel and he finally lets the sparks fly.

But before they can ride off into the sunset, trouble brews and Scout is taken by an enemy from their past that neither of them knew had been waiting for them. Can they overcome this latest hurdle to finally find their happily ever after? Or are they doomed to always be apart?

Book 6:
Tripping Nitro

***Sometimes the one that got away comes
Back... bringing trouble with her.***

It's really her. Former Navy SEAL and member of Charon MC, Nitro can't believe his eyes when he finds his high school girlfriend in a bar nineteen years after she disappeared, taking his heart with her.

Alone and running from a stalker since she was 16 years old, Cindy has avoided all contact with the opposite sex in order to keep her mysterious stalker appeased. Now, with Nitro by her side, he vows to keep both her body and heart protected, but can she risk believing him?

With the help of his Charon MC brothers, Nitro keeps Cindy guarded while he attempts to woo her back into his arms. But just when he manages to break through her walls, she vanishes again. Will Nitro be able to put together all the pieces of the puzzle in time to save his first and only true love?

Book 7:

Scout's Legacy

*There's nothing he won't do to keep those
he loves safe.*

It might have taken Charlie "Scout" Dalton, the president of the Charon MC, over twenty years to see what was right in front of him, but once he did, he didn't waste a moment tying her to him. Now happily married to the love of his life, Marie, they were expecting a baby and had adopted little Ariel. His life was coming up roses.

Once ready to give up on Scout, Marie was now living her dream. Married to the man she's loved forever and carrying his baby in her belly.

But nothing in life ever goes to plan, and the birth of their baby is no exception. An unknown enemy comes to Bridgewater and chaos ensues. In the aftermath, Scout finds his loyalty to everything he holds dear tested. Will he be able to find a way to both save his club and be there for his family?

295

Book 8:
Mac's Destiny

This next club run will change their lives forever.

One day after Jacob "Mac" Miller returns from New York, Scout sends him on another club run. He must go to L.A. and deal with a mob boss who has set his sights on the Charon MC. Sabella is a blast from Mac's past he'd have preferred to leave there, but once he gets word of what the man is now up to, he can't let it stand and willingly leads the charge to go deal with him. Once and for all.

Zara is not happy with the club. Her man just returned from a run up to New York and after only one night home, he's back on the road, leaving her alone with their 10 month old daughter again. It wouldn't be so bad if little Cleo wasn't ill and getting worse.

Circumstances beyond their control test both Mac and Zara as their lives get changed forever in the aftermath of this latest drama that hit the Charon MC.

296

Book 9:
Losing Bash

Life has never been easy for Jake "Bash" Alfonsi, but he's always found a way to survive. Even when his father gave into his PTSD demons and took his own life just days before he turned twenty-one, he got through it. He even managed to go on and find a few slices of happiness in his life. But this latest hand life dealt him is his hardest challenge yet. Will Bash be able to rise once again, or will he get lost in his pain forever?

Book 10:
Finding Needles

In order to find a future, they'll need to put their past behind them.

When Ryan "Needles" Perry left his hometown in Texas as a teenager, he'd had zero intentions of ever returning. But then he never would have guessed that after his father died, his mother would fall for a load of garbage that lands her in one hell of a mess that he needs to come home to clean up.

Elizabeth "Bess" Brooks was Ryan's closest friend growing up and when she finds out his mom is in trouble, she reaches out to tell him. She wants to see his mother safe and will do whatever she can to help, but she vows that it won't include falling for his rough biker charms.

Life hasn't been kind to either of them in the nineteen years since they've seen each other and now they both have secrets that could tear them apart for good, or bond them together forever. But will they survive to find out?